THE WORLD HUNGERS

THE WORLD BURNS - BOOK 3

BOYD CRAVEN

TABLE OF CONTENTS

CHAPTER 1

ANN ARBOR, MICHIGAN, THE DAY THE LIGHTS WENT OUT

When the lights went out, Neal was wandering through the new farmers market downtown. The market had been open for a couple of years, and since he'd moved back to the area for a job, he'd made it a point to visit it again. Neal's job was an IT specialist at the new Michigan State University's College of Human Medicine. He was the one who kept the computers and networks up and running. It wasn't a huge campus, but it shared a parking lot with the market. That's how he found himself buying half a pound of provolone when the lights went out and the cash register quit working.

The register locked, and Neal was unable to cash out. The owner looked at him and then hit a few buttons. He pulled his cell phone out, put the square reader on it, and hit some more buttons. Then he tapped it again, harder.

"It isn't working," he muttered to himself.

The sound of squealing brakes had Neal looking up. He couldn't see what was going on, so he moved around the counter and looked out towards the main aisle and the windows. He heard the crunch of metal, and he looked to the owner again, eyebrows raised in question.

"You know what, I better get back across the street. I'll stop in later for this," Neal told him, backing away from the counter and heading out the door.

He passed dozens upon dozens of people on his way to the front doors and immediately saw two accidents. One was in the market's parking lot, where one car had rolled into another. Across the south side of the parking lot, an MTA bus had collided with another bus at the corner where the bus terminal was located. Neal ran across the lot to the university and immediately noticed all the lights were out inside.

"I need to check on the backup USPS's," he muttered to himself, running to the elevators. He hit the button, but the call light didn't turn on.

"The power's out," a security guard said as he approached Neal from his place near the door.

"I figured as much." Neal jammed the button again out of spite before walking towards the staircase.

He took the stairs two at a time to the third floor,

then slowed as he started to run out of steam. Having a top-floor office had appealed to him before, but having to hoof the stairs only reinforced the fact that he'd been neglecting going to the YMCA that was right down the road from his apartment, actually on the way to the market and work, truth be told.

"I'll worry about exercise later. I don't want to reboot everything," he said, talking to himself again.

Having all the machines lose power at once would mean half a day of getting everything up and running again, and it wasn't something he was looking forward to doing. He dropped his backpack at the doorway to his office and ran the rest of the way to the server room at the back of the floor. He used his keycard and waved it at the lock, waiting for the familiar click, but nothing happened. He tried again and again before he realized it wouldn't work. He put his hand over the handle of the server room and hesitated. He made up his mind, pushed the handle down, and opened the door.

He knew the electronic locks must have opened due to the power being cut, but what about the backup generators? There should be some emergency lighting or something, he thought as he walked into the dark room.

The door closed behind him, and the dark was absolute. No light filtered in from anywhere, and the server racks on the left side of the room weren't lit at all.

"What the hell?"

He fumbled in the darkness, finally finding the doorknob and opening the door. He hadn't realized just how dark the windowless room would be, and even in the hallway, small amounts of light seeped in just enough illumination so that he didn't trip over his own feet. He slowly walked back to his office, noticing all the open doors in the hallway. The employees from the enrollment department looked back at him as he passed.

"Neal?" a booming voice called out from the darkness at the doorway before his office. It was his boss, Mr. Caruthers.

"Yes, sir?"

"Just getting back from your lunch?"

"Uh, yes, sir. The power went out before I got something to eat. I'm not late, am I?"

"Late? I don't know. My phone and watch aren't working. I was going to ask you if the backup generator was running."

"No, I don't think it is. The emergency lighting is out too," Neal said, stating the obvious.

"Well, I'm going to keep folks here till about four p.m. if the power doesn't come back on. If it does, how long until you get the computers up and running again?"

"The computers will come back online immediately, as should the internet. Email, databases, and our internal network may take a few hours."

"You don't mind the overtime, do you?" Mr. Caruthers asked him.

"Naw, but if the power is going to be out, I'd like

to take off about four."

"That's fine by me. You going to hang out in your office, or meet up with the rest of us on the first floor?"

"I'd rather stick around up here, if that's ok," Neal told his boss.

"It's fine by me. I understand completely."

"Thanks."

He hurried to his office and shut the door, closing himself off from the world.

"How am I going to know when four o'clock is?" Neal asked his empty office.

His question was almost immediately answered as the bell tower at St. Matthews rang one p.m. He nodded and sat down at his desk, opening a drawer and pulling out a binder that detailed how to reset the entire system. Since the college had come online, the servers had never all gone down at once. Re-integration shouldn't be too bad; Neal had learned from some of the best minds in the field.

For half a heartbeat, he considered heading down to the cafeteria, but he discarded that idea almost immediately. Neal had always hated being in crowds. Crowds or large groups of people made him break out into a cold sweat and his body tense up. His boss knew this, but he still had reached out. That meant a lot to Neal, because most people just assumed he wanted to be left alone, and they did so. It was a lonely, solitary life, but he didn't have much room for anything else.

Computers, math, chemistry, logic. Those were

environments he knew how to control, and his new job at the university had helped him out a ton. For the first time in his life, he had everything he needed at his grasp. His apartment was six blocks away from his job, his bank at the halfway mark. He bought food as he needed it by walking to the bus station and taking it to the Franklin and Davison supermarket, then riding the bus home. The rest of his transportation consisted of a mountain bike that he'd outfitted with fenders and an attachment behind his seat that bolted on and allowed him to carry a milk-crate-sized portion of cargo.

A backpack and whatever he could fit on the bike rack usually lasted him a good week or more. Neal never learned to drive and never expected to. Life was good. Now? He considered taking his bike for a ride later on instead of his usual night of *Skyrim* or the newest *Call of Duty* game. He could take the main roads to the west side of Saginaw Street and head through some of the lesser populated neighborhoods along Church, Beach, and further down Twelfth Street by the farm. Or he could ride to the river, a place that was almost always vacant for some reason.

He pondered this and read the binder until he started to drift off. He came to with a gentle hand nudging his shoulder.

"All this excitement has you worn out, huh?" Mr. Caruthers smiled.

"I'm sorry, I must have nodded off. What time is it?" Neal's heart raced from being startled awake.

THE WORLD HUNGERS

"It's a little after four. As you can tell, the power isn't back on…you live close by, don't you?"

"Yeah, Court and Lapeer."

"We're going to close the university down until we can figure out the power situation. We've had maintenance trying to figure out the generators and the phone systems. Those are run through your department, aren't they?" Mr. Caruthers asked.

"Yeah. Without power to the servers, the switches from the T3 lines—"

"That's Greek to me. The other problem is the phones. Cell phones even. Nobody's phone seems to work. So I have no way of calling folks back in to work…if the cars would even start, and they haven't yet. So when the power comes on at your place, head on over this way. I'll make sure to have human resources leave time cards out until you can get the network back up."

"Ok, thanks. Wait, cars aren't working?"

"No. No one here has been able to get theirs to start. No one across the street can get theirs working either. You're lucky you live close."

Neal rubbed the sleep from his eyes and grabbed his backpack as he headed out the door, his head fuzzy from the unintentional nap. He waved goodbye to the rest of the folks in the lobby and turned towards the market, intending to cut through parking lots to get home quickly. A puttering noise caught his attention, and he looked towards the front of the market where a small crowd had gathered around what looked like a three-wheeler pulling a small trailer. It was on the sidewalk, next to the glass doors.

For once, he ignored the feelings of panic and approached the crowd, being careful to stay outside of the large mass of people. Security guards and market personnel were soon dispersing the crowd, and everyone left, muttering questions about how the three-wheeler was still running when many of them were stranded with dead cars.

"Do you need help pushing that?" Neal asked, surprising himself.

An armed woman with raven black hair was sitting on the quad, and a vaguely familiar man was pushing the trailer through the double doors of the market and towards a stall.

"Sure. Just…stay away from the three-wheeler. My wife is nervous enough."

"No problem." Neal picked up the end of the trailer and helped push it into the main aisle, stopping at one of the stalls.

"Do you need anything from here?" the man asked him.

"The cash registers don't work."

"Oh, I was going to hook you up for helping. I'm cleaning my stall out, so whatever I can't fit…"

"Cleaning it out?" Neal stepped back once he let go of the trailer.

"Yeah, we're closing down our stall. I'll give you a good deal on some…Hey! Are you Neal Karaway?"

"Yeah, do I know you?"

THE WORLD HUNGERS

"Yeah, my little brother went to Ellen Knopf with you."

Memories came crashing back to Neal, and he recognized the man now. It was Shane's older brother, the one who took care of him. He couldn't quite remember his name.

"Jeff." He held out his hand and smiled.

Neal just looked at it and shook his head.

"I'm Neal. Sorry, I don't touch…"

"I forgot. It's ok. Do you have food stored at home, or somewhere else to go?"

"I haven't gone to the store yet this week…"

"Let me help you stock up."

"I don't have any room to carry…"

He stopped and gaped as the raven-haired woman pushed the quad inside of the building and started to hook it back up to the trailer.

"Hey, who's your friend?" she asked.

"This is Neal Karaway. He was in Shane's class."

The woman appraised Neal and then held out her hand. "I'm Janet."

Neal shook his head and opened his mouth to explain.

"Jan, Neal doesn't like big groups of people. High functioning autistic like Shane, if I remember correctly?" Jeff looked at Neal, who was nodding.

"I remember now. School must have been tough for you."

"School always put me on edge. There were always too many people there."

"Oh, that's ok. I won't hurt you." She smiled.

BOYD CRAVEN

Her eyes were kind. "Do you still stay with your parents?"

"No, they passed away last year. I've got my own place now," Neal replied, relaxed.

"You have enough food there?"

"I haven't gone shopping this week," he repeated.

The couple exchanged glances, and Janet nodded to Jeff.

"Help us load some stuff up, and we'll drop you off with some food. If you can leave the city, that would be better," Jeff said.

"I don't have anywhere else to go," Neal said, confused. "Why would I need to leave town?"

He helped them unload boxes and bags from behind the counter, and large heavy sacks from under a bulk food dispenser shelf onto the trailer.

"The city will probably be safe until the water stops. Then things are going to get ugly," Jeff told him.

"Why would the water stop?"

"The power's out. We got hit by an EMP or a coronal mass ejection. I'm at least ninety-nine percent sure of that."

"You know what that is, don't you?" asked Jan.

"I'm autistic, not retarded," Neal said, a hint of annoyance in his voice.

"I'm sorry, it's just that most people don't know what that means. I didn't mean it like that."

"Sorry. It's just that this whole mess has me worried, and now the world is ending? Is it war?"

THE WORLD HUNGERS

"I don't know, but I didn't mean to offend you. I'm sorry," she told him, a smile tugging at the corner of her mouth.

That made sense to the quiet man, and he just nodded and gave her a rare smile before loading some more bags. He noticed right off that some of the retail-sized bags that were already packaged were going into three boxes and not with the rest of the supplies. These were loaded last on the trailer, and when they were done, they loaded up the cleaning supplies.

"The bleach goes with him," Jeff told his wife, who nodded.

"Do you know how to sterilize water?" asked Neal.

"No, I just turn the sink on and..."

"No, not that. The water is going to stop flowing. Store as much as you can before it goes out. If you have to start drinking river water, and I hope you don't...put it in a container and let the particles all settle to the bottom. Pour that water out, leaving the sediment. Then take this bleach and count out eight drops per gallon of water. If you can't filter the water or let it sit for a while, add twice as much. Shake it up to make sure the bleach mixes and then open the top and wait a half an hour. It tastes like ass, but you won't die from drinking bad water."

"Bleach in the water? I guess that'd work. Never thought about it, and I minored in chemistry. Do you think things are going to get that bad?"

"Yes. It would be better if you just left town,"

Jeff said.

"I really don't have anywhere to go," Neal replied.

"I know, but remember, you have half a million people around here who don't either. Soon they will be hungry, thirsty, or have some sort of axe to grind. I'd hate to think you were here when things get ugly."

"You really think it was something like an EMP?" Neal asked.

"I do. My quad runs because it's so old there's nothing I have to worry about getting fried."

"How long until you think things are going to get scary?"

"Two to three weeks tops. I don't know if you'd want to stick around any longer than that. The government will start to bottle things up, and FEMA camps will start—"

Jan shook her head at her husband. "That's enough, Jeff. We don't want to scare him with some of your frightening conspiracy theories. I do agree that this is really, really bad."

"Ok, ok. Can we at least give you a lift home?"

"I can walk. I live real close."

"You can't walk and carry all these." Jeff pointed to the three boxes and a big brown bag.

"That's too much," Neal shot back. "I didn't help that much."

"Listen, I really wish I could take you with us. I'm taking Shane, but I just don't have enough room for where we're going. If I can give you a month's worth of food and some quick advice, I won't feel so bad driving away."

"You're going home?"

"No, I'm going to our shelter. I won't be back."

"Wow. You must think this is pretty bad."

"It's the end of the world as you know it," Janet said.

Neal couldn't tell if she was being serious, or just trying to make him laugh.

"Hop on back," she continued. "Where do you live?"

He told them and then climbed on the back of the trailer. Jeff and Janet drove the three-wheeler out of the market, a security guard holding the doors open for the three of them. The drive to the apartment building was six blocks, but it took less than a minute for them to weave through stalled traffic.

"Thanks," he said, trying to load his arms up with everything and failing.

"Hun, you want to watch the three-wheeler, or do you want me to?"

"You help him. It'd be my luck he lives on the top floor."

"I do," Neal said, wondering why it mattered.

"Ouch, sorry hun." She smiled and let Jeff off, then sat back down on the quad and turned off the motor.

"This is going to hurt," Jeff muttered.

It took two trips, but they carried everything up and placed it all on the small dining room table.

"I wish I could stay, but I can't. I really hope you get out of town, man. Things aren't going to be safe after a while."

"I'll be ok," Neal told him.

"If you're sure. Take it easy, man. I'll see you someday, I hope."

"Say hi to Shane for me."

"Will do."

Neal shut the door, wondering how much of what he heard from Jeff and Janet he should believe. He was scared they were correct. He had studied the effects of an EMP briefly in his college education—how such an event would burn out the electronics in complicated systems. All modern electronics were complicated, so it would fry everything. Mostly a footnote in his education really, but he considered everything he'd seen and heard from Shane's older brother.

No Power.

No land lines—those were self-powered.

Cell phones weren't working.

Modern cars weren't running.

Evidence suggested Jeff was correct. Neal didn't have anywhere to go, and if Jeff was right, things could get ugly. With nowhere to go, he considered his options. The city had three murders last week alone, one alarmingly close to his apartment, two others in the north end of the city. Muggings and strong-arm robberies were common, but as long as you were smart and aware of the situation, you could stay out of harm's way. Painfully sensitive of being around people, Neal kept an eye on everything, and had always crossed the street or avoided groups of people huddled up together, loitering around. He could take care of himself physically; he just didn't like crowds and the noise associated with them.

Now, the police were probably in the same boat as everyone else. No radios, no cars, and their Tasers were probably dead. Only their guns and batons would still be in working order. Would the police department continue to work if things got bad? Or would the cops stay home and protect their families? How would they communicate? Ann Arbor long held the distinction of being a rough and tough melting pot of people, but it was what he was used to. It was what he grew up with and it was his home. Now it might become his grave. With nothing else to do and too nervous to go out on his bike, he pulled out one of his favorite books and started to go through it. It showed the old abandoned rail lines that criss-crossed the state. He sometimes walked and hiked them, glorifying in the quiet and serenity.

He could walk along one line for more than a day without seeing another human being, and that was the kind of relaxation his mind needed after living in a city crammed full of noise, fumes, and of course, people. He studied the maps and rail lines and drifted off to sleep as the evening wore on. He dreamed about one of his last trips. He'd tried a new spur, and that included going down a used track, leaving his normal route. When the old man stepped out and waved hello, it startled him so badly he'd almost fallen over.

With a chuckle, the old man hobbled up and offered Neal a hand.

"Sorry 'bout that, son. Figured you for another lost kid."

"No, I'm not lost. Thanks for helping me up," Neal said, shouldering his pack and readjusting the weight.

"Not lost? You don't look like no hobo like me and my friends."

"Hobo? You?"

"Yeah, lord of the rails, answer to no man but myself."

"Is that like being homeless?"

"Just because I ain't got no specific home doesn't make me homeless, son. I got lots of homes. Lots of places to stay."

"Oh, well, I'm going to head back now," Neal said, starting to turn.

"You don't like people much, do ya? I can't say I blame you. That's why I moved away from the city."

Something about that statement struck a chord, and Neal turned around.

"I'm agoraphobic. People bother me. Big groups of people."

"That's a fancy word for not liking people, isn't it?" the hobo said, chuckling.

"Yeah, I suppose so." A smile tugged at the corner of Neal's lips.

THE WORLD HUNGERS

"Well, I won't bother you. You ever want to get away from it all and talk to somebody just like yourself, come find old Hobo Bob."

"Okay, maybe I will," Neal murmured. He headed back towards the direction he had come from.

He'd run into Bob again. Just last week, he'd ridden his bike out there, and spent a whole twenty minutes talking to the old man. It was progress. It was stepping outside of his comfort zone, and—

A hard knocking woke him up…

CHAPTER 2

THE HOMESTEAD, KENTUCKY

The thrashing between their bodies woke Blake up. He sat up, rubbing his eyes in the darkness as a small form wrapped his small arms around him and tear-streaked eyes pressed against his chest. Sandra still snored softly in her sleep.

"Shhhh, was it a bad dream?" he whispered.

"The bad man. Are you sure he's gone?"

"He can't hurt you, little buddy."

"Are you sure?" His voice was small and sounded hopeful in the dark bedroom.

"I made sure of that. He can't come here and hurt you."

"Promise?"

"I do. Now, let's get you back into your bed." Blake cradled Chris's small form to his chest as he rose and crossed the room to put the precious bundle onto a custom-made rope bed patterned after the ones in the barn's basement.

"Are you and Ms. Sandra my new mommy and daddy?"

"If you want us to be," he told Chris. They'd spent some time discussing this in private, and the boy's question confirmed what they had thought. He needed safety and stability; something they were more than willing to give to him freely.

"Ok." Chris pulled his blanket over himself and rolled on his side, snoring almost instantly.

Blake sat on the edge of the bed for a long while trying to see if he was tired or not, and in the end he got up, dressed, and headed out of the bedroom, closing the door behind him. He headed to the kitchen with soft footsteps, mindful of the new tenets sleeping in the basement, not wanting to wake them up with a creak or a heavy tread.

"You couldn't sleep either?" Lisa asked him as he entered the kitchen to the smell of coffee.

Blake looked around. Martha was there too, dark spots under her eyes.

"Chris had a nightmare. What are your excuses, ladies?"

Blake sat at the table and accepted an empty cup and the handle of the percolator. He poured himself a cup of the bitter brew and sighed as the hot coffee warmed him.

"It's Duncan," Martha said.

"Is he ok?" Blake was in a panic from the way

the ladies were looking at him.

"Yes, but not for long. He's been out of his medication since the lights went out," Lisa answered.

"He didn't say anything…"

"I doubt he would," Martha said. "He's been having chest pains. Ever since the day that Melissa and that boy came up here."

"I saw him rubbing his chest and asked him," Lisa cut in, "and he admitted he's been out of it."

Blake was relieved, somewhat.

"There's a ton of herbal remedies I know of for that. Hibiscus, French lavender, hawthorn—"

"That may help some, but he needs medication. He's got a little more severe case than that," Martha said. "If we can get to my place, my clinic should have some…"

"Your clinic?" Blake interrupted.

"Yeah. Martha's the vet I worked for." Lisa smiled at her old friend.

"My clinic had all kinds of stuff in it that I think the homestead could benefit from."

"Well then, when it's safe…"

"I don't know if we can wait that long, but let's get your herbal stuff going on him. I want him on a low-salt diet, and he has to eat less—"

"Lisa, we're all on a low-salt diet, but yes, we'll talk to Duncan. I'll get Sandra to sit on him if that's what it takes."

"You tell your wife to work with her ladies squad. I'll sit on him if need be," Lisa said with a straight face. Blake and Martha's jaws dropped open. "I mean, I'll make him behave," she stammered. "I'll...you two quit looking at me like that!"

Lisa turned a furious shade of red as she sputtered. It was an open secret that she had had her hat set on Duncan for a while now. Duncan knew, everyone else knew, but Lisa never acknowledged it or talked about it. She would just let her emotions overtake her from time to time, and her love for the big preacher would overcome her good senses. They all sat in silence after that, watching the sun rise in the east and drinking their coffee.

It had been two days since the rescue, and folks were just starting to settle down. Weston and Bobby had moved out to the barn's "barracks" as everyone started calling it, finding the lack of privacy worthwhile for helping keep the former victims feeling safe and secure. Bobby's case was more to be closer to Melissa, but that was another one of those open secrets that nobody talked about. Weston was there to help make those folks feel secure. He still looked the part of a police officer, and having him around kept the ladies who formed the new "squad" feeling safe and secure. Not enough that they felt comfortable around all men, but they trusted Blake and Weston implicitly.

It was a strange dynamic that held the victims of the slavers together, a shared horror and victory. The other side benefit of having Weston and Bobby there was to get to know the survivors, feel them out for skills that they could put to better use rather than just pulling weeds or keeping a lookout. It had been two long days, much of it spent at a frantic pace. They had finished moving the last camper to the homestead. Instead of torching it, they stripped it and parked it by the old grain silo at the back of the property next to the one Duncan had been sleeping in previously.

The issue of where to store all the firearms had become a problem; especially now with kids on the homestead. In the end, they were hung up out of reach all around the house, locked in the one bedroom, and also stored in the barn's barracks. All the bulk ammunition was stored in the barracks as well, high off the ground on shelves that Bobby had built. It wasn't a perfect solution, but it kept the main stores hidden and safe. Mostly.

The base unit radio was hooked up in the living room of the main house, so the solar array could charge or run it, and it was kept on constantly. That's what the ladies and Blake were listening to as the sun rose, and with it, Sandra. It was so silent that they could hear her roll out of bed and make quiet shushing noises to Chris before she came out and joined them.

"Good morning," she whispered to them, breaking the silence and kissing Blake on the cheek.

"Morning," the three of them chorused.

"I'm taking the squad out for a quick warm-up. Then we're going to work on…" she tapered off, looking at the solemn faces staring back at her.

"What?"

"Your dad's out of his medicine," Blake told her

quietly.

"What?" Sandra asked.

"Martha and I were talking about what I have at her clinic that would work," Lisa said.

"Make's sense. Hun, I'm going to take one of the trucks. You coming with me?" Sandra asked.

"Wait, where are you going?" Blake asked.

"Change of plans. The squad and I are going to Martha's. I assume you're coming as well, Martha?"

"Damn right I am," Martha said.

"Me too." Lisa stood up.

"Well, yeah. We can have Duncan and Weston keep everything on track," Blake said, amused how his wife always took charge of the situation.

"Yeah, and Bobby and one of the men can sit on David and try to make contact with the guard unit. Dad had some interesting ideas on using some misinformation."

"Will David go along with it?" Blake asked.

"He better, or your wife's ladies-only squad will neuter him."

Blake chuckled at that, but quickly noticed none of the women were amused. He cut out the humor that had caught his funny bone.

"Who's going to watch Chris?" Sandra asked.

"I can ask Melissa. Her family was helping to take care of him, you know…before."

"Sounds good. Let's take the big trailer, that way we can fit everyone."

"Blake, Sandra, if we take the big caged trailer, I'd like to make a side trip."

"Where?"

"To a farm that's on the way. I noticed that we don't have any livestock here, and if the Andersons aren't there…"

"What if they are?" Blake asked.

"They aren't. The slavers, they—" she couldn't finish.

"Ok, we'll stop there. Let's get everyone up. I don't want to do this in the middle of the day when everyone is going to be out and about."

"Amen to that," Lisa muttered. They all had a quick smile at that.

"Mom, what's for breakfast?" Chris padded out in his sleeping outfit—sweats with three layers of socks.

Sandra's jaw dropped open and she scooped him up, tears in her eyes. "Anything you want, sweetie."

CHAPTER 3

ANN ARBOR, MICHIGAN, NEALS KITCHEN

Neal startled awake at the knocks. With his heart pounding, he checked the peephole and saw his neighbor, Patty, banging away at it. Either sweat or tears were pouring down her cheeks.

"Please Neal, please," she pleaded, her voice cracking in fear as she looked over her shoulder.

"Oh alright," Neal mumbled to himself. He lifted the security latch, then undid the chain and both deadbolts before opening the door.

Patty rushed in and closed his door in a hurry, then started locking it up. Neal stepped back and away from the door. The raw fear she was exuding had him instantly on edge. He looked around.

"I need to hide here. Please? I know you don't know me well, but they're after me."

"Who's after you?" he asked her after a pause.

"Some of the students. You wouldn't believe me if I told you."

"What did you do?"

She let out a surprised bark of laughter.

"Nothing. I'm a girl, I have blonde hair. I don't know what I did, but they want to hurt me."

"I'm having trouble understanding. I just woke up."

"I was waiting around to see if any of the busses were going to run. A group of Arabic students saw me and immediately started asking me about my faith, my religion."

"Why would they do that?"

"I don't know. I don't know anything about their religion. They were really pushy and kept getting in my face about it."

"Oh."

"When I told them I didn't really practice any faith, they got angry and told me I needed to convert to Islam. We argued, and one of them tried to grab me. I kicked him in the balls and ran. They've been chasing me halfway across the south end of the city."

"Did they see you come in here?"

"Yeah, but I didn't recognize any of them, so I don't think anybody would have a keycard for the front door."

"The power is off, the keycard lock wouldn't work…"

"Oh shit…"

THE WORLD HUNGERS

Footsteps pounded up the stairs, and five dark-skinned figures rushed through the hallway, shouting to each other in a language neither of them understood. They began banging on doors, screaming in another language, and yelling Patty's name.

"How do they know your name?"

"I don't know."

"You should hide. The bathroom has a good lock." Neal told her, more wanting to put some distance between them.

"What are you going to do?"

"I'm going to wait here," he told her, picking up a broom with a wooden handle that was leaning against the wall that separated the front door and the kitchen.

"What if they get in?"

"They won't. Now be quiet and go hide."

Neal was thankful when she left the room, and he put the broom back down and put his eye back to the peephole, watching as the young men ran from door to door and banged on it until the occupants would open the door a crack.

"Patty, girl, blonde hair. You see?"

"No, I haven't seen Patty today. Why are you guys making all this noise? Should I call security?" Old Mrs. Simpson asked from across the hallway.

"No phones. Patty not here?"

"For the last time, I haven't seen her."

"She live this floor?"

"Why do you care? I think I'm going to call security, I don't know you guys."

BOYD CRAVEN

She tried to slam her door, but two men threw their body weight against the door, reaching their hands inside and screaming incoherent words. Everything was muffled behind the closed door, but it was still audible. An eye looking into the peephole startled Neal, and he jerked his head back from the door as he heard surprised expressions of pain. Somebody else banged on the closed door, and the handle jiggled.

Bracing himself and swallowing a big helping of fear, he looked into the peephole as somebody moved their head away, and he could see what looked like half a dozen figures surrounding his door now. The knocking and banging intensified until someone drew back and began viciously kicking the door. They didn't know it, but Neal had researched the construction of the apartments. One of the reasons he felt safe leaving the home he grew up in after his parents' death was how this building had been put together with safety in mind. His doorway had a steel frame, and steel over wood doors. Nothing short of a battering ram would take it off its hinges. And then there were the additions he had made...

Neal grabbed the precut two-by-fours that sat behind the door. He placed them over it, inside the brackets that were drilled deep into the wood that the steel casing was set into. Heavy lag bolts held things together, and with three two-by-fours bracing the door, even a battering ram would have a hard time getting through. He heard a surprised

30

exclamation and looked out through the peephole.

"What do you want?" he yelled through the door.

That startled several of the men on the other side of the door.

"Patty there?"

"Patty who?" Neal asked coyly.

"I know she live here. We need speak her."

"She doesn't live here, this is my place. I don't even have a dog. I don't like pets."

"Where she live?"

"I don't know a Patty. How do you know you have the right place?"

"She lost shoe!" Another one held up a Nike angrily.

"She have live here, only 2 doors we don't see people."

"I think you have bad information. Check the stairwell at the other end of the hallway."

"More than one stairwell?"

"Well yeah, there's one on each side of the building. Maybe the person you are looking for came up one side and then tricked you and went down the other?"

"No trick, she there."

"I told you, I live alone. I don't have anyone else living here with me."

"Neighbor there said she hasn't seen Patty," he said. The man pointed, his features hard to discern. He was of Middle Eastern descent, his words clipped and hard to decipher.

"I don't socialize. I don't like being around people. You guys need to leave."

"Why leave? Patty hurt me. Whole world different. Great Satan has been brought low. I have my revenge."

"I don't know about your revenge, but there isn't a Patty that lives here." Though true, it wasn't what the man had been asking.

"Pssst." Neal turned to see Patty step out of the bathroom. He looked at her feet.

Sure enough, she'd lost a shoe, but she was pointing towards the window in the bathroom. He didn't want to turn his back on the door, but he did and walked towards the bathroom. He saw two uniformed police officers walking down the sidewalk, looking up towards the building. Neal ran to the balcony and stepped out the sliding glass doors.

"Hey, I need help up here!"

The policemen looked up and saw Neal waving frantically.

"What apartment?"

"Five forty-seven. These guys are trying to kick in my door."

They didn't say anything else, but took off for the front door at a dead run. The corner of the apartment building prevented him from seeing anything more. When he turned, Patty was standing by the side of his front door, the broom handle in her hands again. By the sound of things, the men were trying to kick in Neal's door with a fevered pace, the booming sound echoing across the whole apartment. The men surly heard Neal's call for help, and they must have been trying to get in before the cops could get up there.

"She must be here."

"Maybe she's in the other door," a darker skinned man with a slender build hissed.

"I hear someone," one of them whispered, sounding tense.

Neal backed away from the door as heavy footsteps could be heard rounding the corner. He looked at Patty, who shrugged, her eyes wide.

"Police. Freeze!"

"Gun!" a new voice shouted.

Gunshots rang just outside the doorway. There was a heavy thud followed by the sound of people crying out in pain. Patty shoved Neal aside as she rushed to look through the peephole.

"Two police officers. Three men down hard, one being cuffed. The other one is fighting with the second cop."

"What did you really do to them?" Neal asked her in a quiet, horrified voice.

He hadn't bought the story that it was merely a disagreement on religion, but he could understand just a passing anger at being kicked. He normally wasn't a judgmental person, but he was now seriously wondering what she had done.

"Police. Are you alright in there?" a loud voice asked, free of any accent.

Neal got in front of the peephole and looked. Blood was spattered along the wall across from him, and two groaning suspects lay face down with the other burly cop holding their handcuffed hands, a knee on each of their lower backs.

"Yes, I'm fine."

"Is the lady in there with you? The one these guys were looking for?"

"Patty?"

"Yeah, I think so."

"There isn't a woman living here named Patty," Neal said, not lying, but not giving all of the information out freely.

"We have to handle this. Everything is messed up right now, no cars, and no radios. We're going to walk these guys down to the station. We'll be back after that."

"What about the bodies?" Neal asked, seeing the growing stains on the wood floor of the hallway.

"We'll figure it out. One of us will be back later to take your statement. If that lady is around, tell her we need to speak to her."

"Ok, just…don't leave the dead right outside my door, please?"

"We'll drag them out of the way."

"Great, just great," Neal muttered, running his shaking hands through his hair and sitting down on the couch.

He sat there staring at Patty, wondering if she'd ever get around to answering his earlier question. Her face looked odd to him, and after a moment, he realized it was her makeup streaking from the tears. Great silent sobs wracked her body, and Neal tensed. He knew she needed comforting, but he was scared. It wasn't that she was a stranger, he'd seen her around when he was moving in. It was the whole contact. The intimacy of the situation. His entire life was spent shutting that side of himself down so he could function, to maintain a status quo with his own warring emotions. Even if he couldn't express them the same way others could, he had them. They were just locked down deep. One last look at Patty, and the small part of himself he was warring with cracked. Neal stood.

Patty looked up at Neal in fright. She knew he was a quiet man. She'd also heard the rumors that he didn't socialize, go out, or have company. Some rumors from other tenets were even less kind than that. It took her one or two conversations with him, brief ones, to realize that Neal just operated differently than other folks. She knew instinctively that he wasn't one who knew how to express himself and was more than likely autistic. She was correct on all accounts, but his sudden movement scared and shocked her; it was unexpected.

She watched him as he slowly made his way to where she was standing and patted her shoulder.

"I'm so sorry, Neal. I didn't want to get you involved in this." She sobbed again, all the pent-up fears coming out in waves.

Neal pulled her close and patted both shoulders. He looked at her, hoping it was enough, knowing it wasn't. Patty buried her head into his chest and pulled his arms around her. She squeezed him in the middle, and her body shook as everything came out. Neal stood very still, his heart racing. He was trying not to panic. When she finally calmed, she headed to the bathroom and blew her nose and wiped the streaked makeup off with tissue. When she came back out, Neal had fallen asleep on the couch. She sat there in the darkness and eventually moved close to him, letting his warmth comfort her.

§ § §

When the police came back, it awoke the both of them and Patty moved quickly away from Neal and checked the peephole.

"It's the same two cops from before."

"Let them in," he said, rubbing his eyes and moving to a chair in the corner, the furthest place away from everyone he could sit in the dark.

"Hi, are you Patty?"

"Yes Officer, you are?"

"I'm officer Troy Black; this is my partner, Gary Keeton."

"Thank you for helping us out," Patty said, closing the door behind them and putting the bars back in place after running all of the locks.

Neal noticed something about her movements right away. She locked the door and barred it without him asking, taking charge of the situation. When he'd woken up, she'd moved away quickly. She wasn't pushy, but she was taking charge in small, subtle ways and he didn't mind. It saved him from having to get close.

"That's impressive," Officer Black said, looking at the door.

"Steel cased, steel over wood with extra barricade bars," Neal said.

"Wow. I'm not sure if those guys could have gotten through all that."

"They could have always kicked a hole through the wall," Neal said softly.

The cops looked at each other, back at Neal, then at Patty in an inquisitive manner.

"Neal here, he's, well, he doesn't get out around a ton of people. He's a nice guy, from what I can tell."

"You mean, you aren't together?" Officer Keeton asked.

"No, she's a neighbor," Neal said.

"So she was here the whole time when those students were kicking in the door."

"You said she didn't live here?" Black said, more of a question than a statement.

He pulled out a notepad and started jotting down notes.

"She doesn't live here."

"But she was here?"

"Yes."

"Then why did you say…"

"Officers, Neal is very literal. No one asked him if I was in here, just if I lived here. He didn't lie. If I hadn't dropped my keys in the stairwell, I'd never have involved him."

"Ok, we'll get to that in a second. So you reside next door?"

"Yes, apartment five forty-nine…"

CHAPTER 4

THE HOMESTEAD, KENTUCKY

Duncan wasn't surprised when Sandra loaded up the squad, requisitioned two of the trucks and one of the trailers, and left him in charge. Ever since he'd been confronted, he felt...relieved? He'd insisted that the squad take two of the handheld radios in case of emergencies, but he wasn't worried. Time and time again had proven that Blake's levelheadedness and his daughter's stubborn nature would always keep them safe. He did worry a bit about taking the new squad of ladies with only two days of training, but Sandra argued that this was real-life training.

With the large group disposed of, and David not knowing of any others operating in the area, he relented and made sure everyone was outfitted with some of the more modern guns they had looted from the slavers. He'd personally gone over and cleaned every M4 carbine and made sure everything was working perfectly before putting them in the pile to be used. The fact that the slavers were so well armed still made his stomach clench when he thought about it, and they had literally dodged the bullet on them.

Somehow, they had been blessed at every opportunity, except for his unfortunate gunshot wound, which was healing nicely, and the pains in his chest.

"I can still be a teacher and armorer," he'd told Lisa when she put him on restriction yesterday and resigned him to easy work. Honestly, he agreed with her.

Truth was, he was in poor shape before the world as they knew it ended. The survival diet had helped things along, just not fast enough. His blood pressure was winning, and the almost 300-pound man pushed his body harder and farther than he'd done in years. The survival diet and added exercise had helped him lose a lot in the past five weeks, but decades of abusing his body were catching up with him fast.

He'd handed Sandra a few of the grenades when Blake wasn't looking as a "just in case" measure, but he didn't think they'd need them. The world had gone quiet, with the exception of the nightly broadcasts on the base station radio. None of them had wind-up clocks, and when the grid went down, their phones and watches became useless, but the radio broadcast claimed they'd be back at 7 p.m. every night. None of the news was good.

Martial law had been enacted, and except for some basic updates, most of the information was looped from the previous day's news. Everyone was told to stay in place; all travel was restricted, and food and medical relief were coming. The United States of America was officially at war, but the broadcast didn't specify with who or what was being done about it. It was malarkey, and everyone who listened to it understood it to be what it was: window dressing that was supposed to make everyone feel better.

"Duncan, I've got the list for you." Weston strode up, handing him a hand-drawn list of names.

"Give me the lowdown."

"Nine women between the ages of eighteen and sixty-five. Seven men ages twenty-seven to fifty-nine, and three boys, Chris being the youngest at six, and the oldest being fourteen. Five girls ranging from nine to fourteen."

"How many of them were abused by those degenerates?" Duncan growled.

"Most," Weston paused and held up a hand as Duncan turned an alarming shade of red, "most of them are actually doing well at the moment. I don't think you going around and raging will help them any. The good news is that one of the older ladies is a psychologist. She's been working with all but Sandra's squad. They were kept separate ever since they were incarcerated in that damned camper."

"If I could kill them again—"

"Then I would do it," Bobby joined the conversation.

"How's your, uh…lady friend?" Weston asked.

"Melissa? Still going from shocked about being rescued to being a complete mess."

"Those girls have been through a lot," Weston said.

"Yeah, we're talking a bit, but her dad doesn't seem to—"

"Dads are like that." Duncan patted him on the shoulder.

"You weren't like that. Not with Blake," Bobby pointed out.

"My daughter, she looks like a pixie, is almost one and a half times your age, and can mop the floor with about any man I've ever met. Blake? I think his laid-back attitude is what keeps my daughter in check. They are perfect for each other."

Bobby groaned out loud.

"What?" Weston asked his brother, jabbing him in the ribs with an elbow.

"Her dad hates me. I obviously don't have parental unit approval."

"She can date when she's thirty," somebody from the back of the barracks yelled, and everyone busted up laughing.

"Does everyone know?" Bobby asked his older brother.

"That you've taken a shine to her? Anyone with eyes."

THE WORLD HUNGERS

After a few more minutes of ribbing, Bobby took a 1911 .45 and an M4, got his camo gear on, and headed down the lane to take watch where Duncan normally sat. It was decided that Weston would watch David today. It was mostly an intimidation factor, as Weston had literally beaten the information out of the former raider once. He'd be more likely to behave with the big cop around. One of the men from the rescue group took a 1911 and two extra magazines and followed Weston and David to the house. Duncan looked at the list and tried to decide what was first.

"The children need their schooling," a matronly woman told him as Duncan sat and studied the list.

"Hi, you're Eva?" he asked her.

"Yes. I used to be a school teacher, but I'm retired now."

"I'm Duncan, Sandra's dad."

"I know. We all do actually." She smiled. "I know you suddenly have a lot of new faces here, but I wanted to tell you how much we all appreciate it."

"Thank you," he said humbly. "How is everyone? I mean, things were bad. How is everyone doing spiritually?"

"Stronger than you'd think, but needing guidance. If only we had a man of God here…"

Duncan smiled. *Teacher, armorer and preacher,* he amended in his head. Even though he had to slow down, he felt good.

§ § §

"Okay ladies, you move like this." Sandra showed them how to move between cover spots.

Soon even Lisa and Blake had gotten the hang of moving from one spot to another, covering each other. It seemed like overkill on the deserted-looking ranch that made up Martha's home, with her clinic on the same property. They moved their way to the house, clearing every room and finding nothing wrong. Then they cleared the clinic and surrounding areas on the dirt road going into her property before moving the trucks and trailer in to start loading things up. Everything from scalpels to catgut stitches to forceps to gauze was loaded. Being so far out in the middle of nowhere, Martha also had her own small pharmacy, and everything from there was lovingly boxed up and packed as well.

They were careful to only load the bed of one of the trucks and part of the caged trailer before Martha called a stop and went inside her house. After a while, Blake and the rest of the ladies stepped inside to check on her. They found Martha in the bathroom, wiping her tear-streaked eyes with a tissue as she looked into the mirror.

"My husband died young. He built this place for me, back in the 1990s. He supported me through school, and now he's gone. It's all gone—" She broke off as sobs wracked her frame.

Lisa was the closest. She pulled her into a tight embrace, and Martha buried her face in her shoulder. Lisa's hair covered Martha's face in a soft cur-

THE WORLD HUNGERS

tain.

"It's time to start over. Everything is different," Lisa whispered.

"I know. I didn't think it'd be so hard coming back here. Now, all I want to do is—"

"Martha, we need you," Sandra said, moving close to Lisa, rubbing the top of Martha's head.

"Why?" She looked up.

"You're the closest thing to a doctor anybody around here has. We need you, and desperately."

Martha sniffed and wiped her eyes before slinging her rifle across her shoulder and walking out the door, her shoulders squared, her head held high.

"Do you think she's going to be okay?" Blake asked Lisa.

"Yes, I just think she was overwhelmed in the moment," Lisa replied.

"Who wouldn't be?" Sandra rubbed Blake's shoulder before exiting the house after Martha.

The squad plus Blake loaded up, the ladies riding in the back of the trucks beds. They held on as the forward momentum rocked them slightly. They were coasting slow, letting the trucks roll in second or third gear to prevent them from being too loud in the now quiet world. Just the sound of the idling motor was loud, but to press on the gas with a perfectly performing muffler was almost as loud as gunfire.

Martha's eyes were still watery as the group eased out onto the country road slowly and made their way back towards the farm. Sandra and Martha were driving the lead truck, leaving Blake to drive the second one pulling the trailer. Lisa sat by his side, keeping him company.

"Did you guys find the blood pressure medicine?" Lisa asked him once everyone had settled down in the cab behind them and she could talk easily.

"Yeah, Martha had something she found that she said would work as long as Duncan can remember his dosage. Good thing he still has an empty bottle," Blake told her, shifting gears as he followed his wife's lead.

"That's a blessing. Do you think it's getting safer out here now? I haven't seen anyone since we left the homestead."

"I don't know if I would call it safe, but I imagine with the groups that have been in this area, everyone has their heads down," he told her.

"Or they're all dead." Her voice was just as quiet.

"Or they're all dead," he agreed.

§ § §

"…what do you mean Charlie and James are dead?" The voice coming through the radio crackled, the static making it hard to hear.

Weston had his arms folded and was looking at David menacingly. "Tell them what we said."

"Something in the food we stole. Whole camp got sick. I'm the only one who didn't get it."

"How did the whole camp get sick, and you

didn't?"

"I was on watch, got back after everyone had eaten. They're dead man, they're all dead."

"What about the others?"

This hadn't been part of the script. Weston just shrugged and pointed at the radio.

"I snuck as close as I dared to. Things are quiet there. I didn't see anyone around."

"Do you think they are dead too?"

David looked at the two men guarding him. If he told the guard unit that they were already dead, they'd want the supplies the homestead had. If he told them that they were alive and healthy, the unit might want to come in guns blazing, ready to take their wrath out on the homestead.

"I don't know. With me being the only one left alive, I was worried that if they were still around, I'd be captured and compromised."

"For a coward, you actually make pretty good sense. Okay then, fall back for now and hole up somewhere. We'll be around your neck of the woods the next time we are making our sweep towards Greenville, and we'll pick up you and the equipment I loaned my favorite nephew. Did any of the women survive at least?"

"Damn it, lie," Weston hissed.

"I'm the only one who lived. I left the bodies in an alfalfa field and moved the trucks and supplies back into the tree line. Do you want me to come to you?"

"No, stay there. The interim governor has us

jumping through hoops, and we probably can't swing through for a couple weeks anyways. So stay put."

"What am I supposed to do for food?" David asked, an inspired question meant to throw off suspicion.

"Hunt, maybe mosey over to the homestead and shake your ass. I think that's what James used Melissa to do, used her as bait to get into some of the fatter targets. You'll think of something. If you didn't have some of our hardware stored for us, we'd probably cut you loose."

"You wouldn't dare…"

"Why not? Charlie is dead. You were always the turd that we scraped off our boots at the end of a long day."

"Go to hell."

"Have a nice life, coward. Maybe we'll see you soon. Maybe we'll let you starve, then piss on your corpse. Gerard out."

David sat back, his face beaded in sweat. His skin was an alarming shade of red and he was sputtering, wanting to stand and stomp and tear things apart. He did none of those things. The bores of the two pistols the men were pointing at him reminded him to keep his temper in check.

"Why do they keep calling you a coward?" Russell, one of the slavers' victims who'd accompanied Weston, asked.

"Because I wouldn't take turns on the women. Because I won't shoot people in the back."

THE WORLD HUNGERS

"But you have killed?" Weston asked.

"Sure, somebody shoots at me, I shoot back. Everyone has killed since the nukes. Thing is, I never executed people. My cousin Charlie on the other hand…"

"Is that why the women always ridicule you?" Russell asked.

"Why, because I won't hit them? It pisses me off, but I'm not gay. I just don't want a woman who doesn't come into my bed willingly. I think the women take verbal shots at me because they know in their hearts I wouldn't have hurt them."

"Then why were you with that group?" Weston questioned him.

"Protection. My cousin always had connections. It's how he had his uncle on his wife's side drop off two crates of weapons for us to 'guard'. They called it pre-positioning."

"Interesting," Weston mumbled, rubbing his chin.

CHAPTER 5

NEAL'S APARTMENT, ANN ARBOR, MICHIGAN

The police took their statements, and he briefly stopped when they heard some noises outside the apartment. It was somebody from the coroner's office, panting and out of breath, who had come to take care of the bodies. They were using candles for light, which gave Neal an idea. He rose to light some before the stink of blood and cordite could overwhelm him from the open doorway.

Neal learned that there had in fact been more to Patty's story, and he could understand why she didn't want to share it. He felt horrible to have heard it, let alone know that a kind woman had to endure the hateful words. One of the survivors had given a statement, and it matched up with what she'd told the police herself. They had done more than question her about her faith; they told her that in their faith, a woman who showed herself the way she did—in a dress and with her hair flowing free—was a slut and treated as such. And since none of them had ever bedded a white woman...Taking a woman by force in their country wasn't looked down upon if it was such a woman.

The cops had narrowed their eyes at that revelation and kept writing long after she had quit speaking.

"Does anyone want anything to drink? I know it won't be cold forever, but I've got some red wine we could share," Neal said, standing.

"I'd rather have a beer, to be honest," Officer Black said, surprising everyone.

"I'll take whatever's cold," Officer Keeton said. "Those stairs were murder getting up after the adrenaline wore off."

"Beck's ok?" Neal asked, opening the fridge.

"Sure."

Neal got everyone their drinks, including a glass of wine for Patty. He marveled at the scene before him. If anyone would have told him a week ago that he'd be having a casual drink with three strangers, two of them cops, another a woman, he would have laughed. Maybe not to their face, but in general. Now? They were discussing the power grid, and things were looking grim.

Both officers had families in the city, and although the event had just happened, the populace of the city was gearing up and things were getting ugly. Both of them were talking about how long the department could hold things together with no communications, no transportation and no way to house and feed the population in the jail.

"But it just happened!" Neal stated.

"Somebody had to have known ahead of time. The guys who attacked your door knew something was up. The one was talking about the Great Satan being humbled and this day has been long awaited…A real smug asshole."

"Have you heard anything from outside the city?"

"No, nothing. Everything just quit working while we were in the squad room getting ready for our beat. Hell, we might have finished our shift and I wouldn't know it." Black held up a wristwatch that had gone dark.

"What do we do?" Patty asked.

"Can you get back into your apartment?"

"I think so, but I'll have to look for my keys or have the office get me a spare set."

"It's the middle of the night? You can have the couch if you want," Neal said, surprising himself and feeling the effects of the wine.

"That's probably a safe bet. Is your door this strong?"

"No." Her voice was small in the flickering candlelight, making her seem fragile and vulnerable.

"I'd take him up on it," Keeton told her as they rose, their hands outstretched.

After a long hesitation, Neal stood and shook

first one and then the other's hand. When the door closed, he turned and was crushed by Patty, who buried her head in his chest again, hugging the air out of his lungs.

"Patty, I can't...I mean, I don't think I—"

"Yes you can." She squeezed harder before letting him go.

"Let's get some rest, then we'll look for your keys in the daylight."

§ § §

They never found her keys, but were able to get a set from the office manager. He lived on the bottom floor and had slept through the entire episode with the cops and the gunfire. He didn't believe Neal and Patty, but followed them upstairs and was horrified at the now brownish stains over the woodwork and walls.

"Oh wow. I'll uh...bring a mop up and..."

Neal opened his door and Patty followed him.

"Neal, thank you. I won't bug you, but I was wondering...?"

"Yeah?" he asked, every part of his body wound up tight.

"Can we be friends? I know so little about you, and I think we both need friends right now. Especially now."

"Yeah, I think so. Just don't hug me without warning me."

"No touch?" she teased, putting a finger out, almost touching his chest.

"No, please," he told her, but a smile was tugging at the corners of his mouth.

"I'm going to get cleaned up. Maybe I can come over later on and I can cook you something. You saved me Neal, and I appreciate it," she told him, not wanting to overdo it.

"It's ok. I just…"

She crushed him in a hug and laughed when his whole body tensed, but he didn't pull away.

"I'll knock first." She slipped out the door and left him alone with his thoughts.

He decided to do the same thing and freshen up, having fallen asleep on the couch sitting up near Patty. He took a shower, and the hot water lasted for a short while, but the warm went cold and then the pressure started to get bad. Remembering what Shane's brother told him, he hurried and shut off the tap and went to the kitchen. He filled glasses, pots, pans, and everything that could hold water, and lined it up on his counters and dining room table. He straightened up the apartment in general and opened the drapes of his sliding glass door to let in the sunlight.

Already, the heat of the summer morning had baked the brickwork outside and the temperature was rising inside. It was still comfortable, but it was going to get warm today. He stepped out on his balcony and smiled as the clean, crisp wind kissed his exposed skin. The only thing that could make the moment better for him was to have his games, but he knew that wasn't going to happen, and part of him was coming to terms with the fact that it would never happen. He tried to focus on the important things: food, water, and safety. Thoughts of Patty kept interrupting him, and he almost jumped when he heard knocking at his front door.

He opened it, and Patty came in. His elderly neighbor, Mrs. Simpson, stuck her head outside her door and gaped at the dried blood stains.

"Is everything okay?" she asked, her voice almost a croak.

"Yes, the police took care of things. Are you ok? Did they hurt you?" Patty asked.

"No, those creeps stuck their hands in the doorway and I wacked them with this." She held up a wooden tee ball bat and gave them a crooked smile.

"They pulled a gun and the cops shot some of them and took the rest away in handcuffs," Patty said.

"I tried calling security, then 911. Everything is dead."

"You know, I'll come over a little later and I'll fill you in on what I know, Mrs. Simpson, but for now...I have to cook for Neal. I promised him a thank-you meal."

"Ok, well, I'll see you both later on then."

Neal closed the door and stepped back as Patty took an armload of groceries into his kitchen.

"You have an electric stove," she said, her voice sounding disappointed.

"Yeah."

"How am I going to cook you dinner on an electric stove?" She sound exasperated.

"I was hoping to find out myself."

"Wait, was that a joke? Did you just make a joke?"

"Yes, sorry. I was just…"

He was pelted in the head by a dish rag she'd snatched out of the sink, but she was smiling.

"I can go get my camp stove. Can you clear me off a space to cook, and then you can tell me why you have water everywhere."

"Sure," he said, watching her go.

He cleared off the stove, putting the glasses and pots of water on his end tables by the couch. He looked into the bag she'd brought. A box of noodles, a jar of pasta sauce, and a half-thawed tube of Italian sausage. His stomach rumbled, making him think back to the last meal he had. It had been almost a day ago, and the adrenaline of yesterday and last night had masked the feelings of hunger. Now that his stomach was awake, it made no mistake in telling him that it needed to be filled. He searched around for a pot that wasn't in use and couldn't find any. He'd probably have to use one to boil the noodles anyways, so he instead looked for a skillet for the meat.

Patty came back within minutes with a small green Coleman stove and had the meal ready in no time. They ate together silently, and when they were done, he wiped the dishes off with paper towels, not wanting to waste the water.

THE WORLD HUNGERS

"Why are you storing all this water?"

"Are you losing pressure in your apartment?"

"Yes, some in the shower. The hot water is out." She shivered at the thought.

"Same here too. Shane's brother told me the water wouldn't stay on long in the city, and that I should store it. He gave me bleach to purify it when it wouldn't come out of the taps anymore."

"Yeah, that works."

"You know about that?"

"Yeah, I spent some time with the Peace Corps when I was younger. Went all over the world. That's how I have all my camping gear."

"He gave me this stuff too," Neal said, showing her all the dried goods.

"Wow, uh, that's enough to last you a month or longer."

"That's what he said, but I don't know how to cook most of it."

"You boil beans," she said with a smile.

"Yeah, but…"

She leaned forward and kissed his cheek.

"Thank you, Neal. For saving me and for being my friend."

"You're welcome."

She sat down next to him and waited for him to relax before holding his hand.

§ § §

It didn't take two weeks for the water to stop, it took

less than one. They had stopped showering after the first week so they wouldn't have to lug wash water up from the river, and although they had a great protected spot at the top floor of the building, water weighs in at twelve pounds per gallon, and that's about the minimum they both needed during the hot summer months. To flush the toilet, they needed almost two gallons of water, which put them up to a four-gallon-a-day minimum needed for their new city life.

During the second week, gunfire broke out as they were filling buckets by the river; they abandoned the buckets and ran. They were able to come back later on and retrieve the buckets and the water, but it had been close. From their balconies they could see the smoke starting to rise from various parts of the city. People no longer walked openly in the streets during the daylight, not without mobs of people going after them or harassing them. Everyone adjusted to a more nocturnal lifestyle, the darkness making everyone appear to be equal.

Officer Black stopped in on his last day of the force. What he had to tell them was disturbing, to say the least. The good people, the families, and those who didn't have an axe to grind left the ruins of Ann Arbor in masses. Twice, groups of people had kicked in the front doors of businesses and apartment complexes close by to rob, loot, and steal at will. The police were out in force, but too little, too late. One officer shot into a mob that was looting. The angry crowd pulled him apart when he ran out of bullets. Other officers quit showing up for work to protect their families. When things couldn't get worse, the city officials that were left made one of the worst decisions that they could have made, in Black's opinion. With no way to house and feed the jail, the order had been given to release the prisoners. Every single one of them.

"Officer Black, you're saying those guys who tried to attack this apartment are now loose?"

"It's even worse than that." He rubbed his head before answering.

"How can it be worse?" Patty asked.

"There's a radical Islamic faction within the prison system. Those two are just the tip of the iceberg. I don't know if you've been keeping up with things, but have you two noticed more fires than usual, gunfire, explosions?"

"Yeah, I can make out quite a bit from the balcony. I didn't know about the explosions. We stay inside most of the time. Safer."

"Those explosions are rare, but it's gotten ugly. What makes those prisoners worse is that they were just the beginning. We had a tactical nuke blow up over our part of the country by ISIS, causing a massive EMP. I don't know how an open secret like this got past the feds, but all the foreign students to some degree knew it was going to happen, along with millions of local radical elements."

"That's a pretty bold statement to make. Is there proof?"

"How about this for proof. What would you say

if I told you that terrorists make up a very small number of folks who practice the Muslim faith?"

"I could agree with that, from what I've read," Patty said.

"What if I told you that the Muslim population in this state supports terrorism against the United States at about eighty-five percent of the time?"

"No, that can't be right," Patty said.

"No, actually, that's an old fact from 2013," Neal told her. "I have no idea what it is now."

"Exactly," Officer Black said. "What I came here to tell you is that I don't want to see you two attacked by a large group. Last I heard about the two we arrested is that they blame the two of you for the deaths of their friends. It's crazy, but they have quite the following. I think they are coming back here."

"I'm not sure I can believe that. It's only been two weeks since the power went out."

"I know. Anecdotal evidence suggests that they've known ahead of time about the attack on the USA and have been waiting. You've now got a target on your backs."

"What does that mean?"

"They're organized. They're starting to execute people in the north end. Convert or die. With their leaders out of jail…" Black's words trailed off.

"Convert?" Patty asked.

"Convert to Islam, or die. Before this happened, it wasn't all that uncommon in the black population up there to have an equal population of Christians and Muslims. If folks were religious, that is."

THE WORLD HUNGERS

"It can't just be the black population," Patty said, horrified at the generalization.

"It isn't. Don't forget the student population. The thousands and thousands of kids in this town alone studying abroad. The two that Gary and I arrested were from Iran and Saudi Arabia. The three dead guys were a mixture as well. It's getting scary out there." He motioned out the window.

"What are you going to do?" Neal asked him, pulling a warm Beck's from the non functioning refrigerator for him.

"Go home, pack my wife and daughter up, and leave the city."

"Where will you go?" Patty asked.

"My folks have a place in the country. I should be able to make it in a week's travel. We'll go on foot if we need to, bike if things are horrible. I don't have much left. What will you two do?"

"I don't know. I don't have any place to go," Patty told him.

"No family?" Neal asked her.

"No. What about you?"

"My parents and grandparents are all dead. I'm an only child."

"If I didn't have any place to go…" Officer Black started to say, but he was interrupted by the sound of a blast. Moments later, there was a rumbling beneath their feet as the building shook. "Oh shit," he muttered, running to the window.

A large group was making its way down Court Street. Someone from the mob threw an object that

61

landed near a car far ahead of them, and the explosion was tremendous. It lifted the parked car several feet off the ground, only to slam down on the pavement in a burning heap. Hoots and cheers were heard over the cacophony of noise.

"I have to go. I'm going to guess the group throwing grenades isn't here for me. If you two want to leave, I've got my service pistol and shotgun still."

"I have to pack," Neal said, thinking of everything he had ready.

"Neal, you have no time. If this is the group that's after you—"

An explosion rocked the lower levels of the apartment complex.

"We have to go," Black shouted, the screams of the folks in the apartments from all levels almost drowning out the sounds.

For two weeks, the world in the apartment had been silent. It was like every tenet had been holding their breath, waiting for things to go back to normal, fearing that it wouldn't. Now the lower level was being attacked, and everyone above the second story was suddenly realizing they had nowhere else to go.

"Ok, let me get my bike," Neal said loudly, but no one was listening.

He grabbed the backpack that Patty had put together for him for this purpose and pulled his arms through.

"Take the south stairs. You need a key to get into the first floor door, so it should be clear," Patty yelled, opening the door to the hallway and rushing out.

"What are you doing?" Black called to her.

"I have to grab something." She was frantically trying to get her key into the lock of her apartment door. "Neal, get the second backpack by the door. I'll meet you on the stairwell."

"I'm not going to leave you behind," he told her, touching her shoulder.

"You have to go. Trust me, I'll catch up to you," she told him over her shoulder.

"But my bike…"

"We don't have time," Black told him, grabbing the pack and throwing it at the IT specialist.

Black nearly shoved Neal through the steel door face first. Neal paused for half a second to get his footing, despite Officer Black's worry. Gunshots made them both flinch, but it became obvious that it was floors below them. The shouts and cries from the lower level made it up the stairwell.

"Go." Black pushed him as he took his shotgun off the shoulder sling.

"I'm waiting for Patty," he said stubbornly, surprising himself.

In the last two weeks, he'd gotten used to her, almost as well as he'd gotten used to Shane at school. Just because he wasn't comfortable and didn't like to be around a lot of people didn't mean he didn't like to be around her. The truth was, he did, and he was racking his brain to tell her but didn't know how.

"You need to move." Black pushed him again, almost making him trip.

Neal stumbled but found his footing, trying to throw the backpack over his shoulder as he rushed to the stairwell. He almost stopped at the thought of all the innocent people, but the gunfire broke his resolve, and he told himself that he'd have to be content to leave his apartment unlocked. He hoped that if the gunmen found him gone, they would leave the rest of the residents alone. He pushed the stairwell door open and chanced a look back. Patty was running out of her apartment with a big framed backpack on, her feet slamming down hard. Neal held the door until Black was through, then pushed it closed as Patty ran.

"Do you want to trade packs?" Neal asked her.

"No, just go," she said, seeing Black pulling his pistol out and heading down the stairwell.

"Are you sure the first floor door locks?"

"Yes, with a key. This is the service stairs."

"There's a fire escape on the second floor," Neal offered.

"Let's go," Black said, taking the stairs two at a time.

They met nobody in the stairwell, and their pounding footsteps were almost drowned out by the sound of their harsh, panting breaths. They stopped at the second story door and Black looked out. The window to the fire escape was straight in front of the door, the hallway stretching to the left and right and out of sight.

THE WORLD HUNGERS

"I'm going to check it out; I'll let you know if it's clear," Black said, pushing the door's bar and unlocking it.

Officer Black stepped out. He looked left, then right, then turned to them, holding the door open for them.

"Come on, it's safe—" His words were cut off by the chatter of gunfire.

His vest stopped two of the bullets, but the third and fourth hit the side of his neck, and the last one took off his head in a red explosion. His corpse fell forward, and both Neal and Patty ducked out of the doorway a moment.

"That cop. He's one of them," a voice called from the hallway.

"The others must be close by. He was talking to them, I know it," a deep voice replied.

Black had fallen halfway into the doorway, and his pistol had fallen when he'd first been shot, but his shotgun was still over his shoulder. Neal grabbed it up and racked the slide quietly, making sure it was loaded. He took the safety off and motioned for Patty to get back into the stairwell behind him. He got back there himself and stepped back onto the third stair and waited. Three men stepped into the open doorway over Black's body, and Neal chambered off two shots from the twelve gauge. The noise in the confined space was deafening, and the cordite stung their eyes and nostrils. It took a moment for the smoke to clear enough for Neal to see all three forms down, the walls around them torn up from the heavy load of buckshot.

"One of them is still moving," Patty whispered, looking over his shoulder.

One more blast rang out, hurting their senses even more. They moved forward. Patty knelt and grabbed a pistol and an AK from one of the bloody corpses. Neal grabbed some shotgun shells from Black and a satchel the other fallen student had carried. They ran into the hallway and to the window. Patty held the sash up for Neal, but he motioned for her to go first. He could hear footsteps running their way and wanted to be able to cover Patty's escape. He was startled when Patty almost dragged him through the window by his belt, but he made his way out. He shut the window slowly, hoping that in the confusion, the attacking group would run up the stairs instead.

"Hurry," Patty begged.

They fled, noticing smoke pouring out of the casing of the first-floor windows. Shouting, gunfire, and another explosion rocked the building. A window blew out somewhere above them, and it only made them hurry even more. Patty jumped the last couple feet to the ground, her heavy pack pulling her off her feet. Neal descended and helped her up, and they hurried out of there. They fled south and west, resting under an overpass to catch their breath.

"Do you know where we should go?" Patty asked him, wiping a stray hair out of her eyes.

"I have an idea," Neal said after a few minutes. "We're heading to the rail line."

CHAPTER 6

KENTUCKY

Hey hun, you still want eggs?" Sandra's voice drifted out of the big barn.

"Yeah, but I thought the coop was empty," Blake called back to her, his gun at the ready.

"They got out. They're in here with the feed."

They had parked the trucks and made their way onto the property. Once it was determined that things were clear, they pulled in, and Blake parked the truck he had been driving close to the barn. The stench of decay was heavy in the air, and Lisa had found the bodies of the family that had lived here. The man had been shot in the forehead and left where he fell, that much was evident on the body. The woman was harder to tell, or she was hurt worse. No one injury stood out above the others, and she'd been left with her dressed pulled up.

The body of a teenage boy had been found last, hanging out the window of the farm house. Bullet holes surrounded the window and inside the room he'd been in. It looked like a terrible gunfight had occurred here, and casings from a 30/.06 littered the floor of the room. It looked as if the boy had taken the fight to the raiders, shooting at them from the cover of his bedroom, but the sheer amount of lead that surrounded the window frame and inside the bedroom almost looked like it had been poured in from all directions.

"Come help me catch them." Sandra's muffled voice floated out from the dark of the barn.

Opening the door, Blake and Lisa stepped in and looked around the hay-filled barn. It took a full minute for their eyes to adjust to the gloom, and they slung their long guns over their backs and entered.

"Wish we had a flashlight," Lisa muttered, moving closer to Blake.

"I know. Where do you think my wife is?" he replied, equally as quiet.

"Up here, guys," Sandra boomed, right over their heads. They flinched and looked up. "Sorry about that. They got up here where the bulk grain is stored."

Sandra was standing on a cross beam, almost fifteen feet above them, smiling.

"We'll be right up," he called back, spotting the ladder.

THE WORLD HUNGERS

Once they reached the level where Sandra was, they immediately heard the soft clucking of hens.

"There they are," Lisa smiled, pointing.

Half a dozen chickens were scratching through the grains that had spilled on the loft's floor. A couple of them were sitting in piles of loose hay.

"One of the hens has babies." Sandra smiled.

"What about the other one?"

"I think she's sitting on some eggs also, but she won't let me sneak a hand under her."

"Because she's probably ready to hatch them," Martha told them, pulling herself up the ladder with a pet carrier.

"What's that for?" Blake asked her.

"For these two hens. The rest can go into the big cage, I guess."

There was an art to catching chickens, and none of them had it. Two of the squad nervously watched the road and the surrounding area while everyone else took off their equipment and chased the zany birds around the barn. Sandra was about to claim victory and hold a bird up high that she'd just caught, when one foot swept out from under her.

"Oooof." The breath went out of her.

"Sandra, are you ok?" Blake asked, trying to hide his smile.

"Did that look as silly as it felt?"

"Feet out from under you, landed flat on your back? Yeah."

"Kind of knocked the breath out of me."

"What did you slip on?"

She held her shoe up and looked at it. A thick, pungent pile of chicken manure had caused the Wile E. Coyote moment, and they all had a chuckle. It wasn't until Lisa had gone downstairs and found a landing net from somewhere that they were able to catch them. Used for assisting anglers to bring in larger fish, the landing net gave them just enough of a reach to get close and finally round up the chickens.

"I don't see any roosters," Martha muttered.

"What's that mean?" Sandra asked.

"That there may be no more eggs once these guys are gone. Unless…"

"Some of these baby chicks are roosters!" Lisa held up the pet carrier.

They decided to leave the broody hen whose chicks hadn't hatched yet and planned to come back on another trip. There were two bulk fuel tanks there, one full of diesel, and the other a mystery. Both ways, there was fuel stalled out alongside the highway everywhere, and the trucks hadn't been topped off in a month. They'd only taken short trips back and forth into town, or to the end of the lane. With their fleet of vehicles slowly growing, it made sense to do something about fuel, and if Sandra's plans for the squad went forward, the ladies would become the forward observers for the group.

They loaded up and were soon headed back to the homestead, weaving their way through the stalled traffic that had become the norm. Five miles from their turn off the highway, closer to the

THE WORLD HUNGERS

burned-out town, they saw two cars pushed nose to nose in the road almost 400 yards ahead of them. Blake almost had to stand on the brake pedal, and he stalled his truck to try to miss rear-ending Sandra's. The ladies all emptied out of the trucks, looking bewildered.

"Get in some sort of cover," Sandra hissed as everybody hustled.

"What is it?" Blake asked her, running low to the ground, keeping the front end of a nearby car between him and the new blockade.

"Somebody's blocked the road."

"I can see that," he said sardonically.

"Quit stating the obvious, what does it—" Lisa's voice was cut off by a gunshot, and a bullet punched a hole into the sheet metal above Blake's head. Everybody dropped to the ground.

"Anybody get a look at where that shot came from?" Sandra asked.

"Northeast. Uh…three o'clock?" Martha asked.

"Who's got a scope?" Blake asked, kicking himself for leaving his deer rifle at home.

It was what he practiced with, and he'd bought into the common gun, common caliber mindset. He flinched when another bullet whizzed by his head. He tried to sink into the asphalt.

"Why are they shooting at me?" he asked his wife, whose lips were pinched. She was scanning the north side of the highway where the sound of the second shot came from.

"They don't want to hurt the women…" She

looked into his eyes, her gaze speaking volumes about the horrors she imagined.

"Here's my gun. Didn't have a chance to sit through Duncan's primer on the M4." Lisa slid a scoped .308 to Blake, who belly crawled so he was just behind the driver's side tire of his vehicle, leaving most of the engine block and front of the truck available to stop the bullet.

Blake scoped the area, but a third shot parted his hair and he rolled under the truck, swearing at the burning sensation at his scalp.

"Sniper," he shouted to his wife, sliding the useless scoped rifle out from the truck.

No shots had come anywhere near the women. Every shot was directed at Blake's head. Sandra immediately made connections in her head. She knew that there was at least two to three men in the group based on the spacing of the shots. One to pin Blake down, the second shot fired from a different position. Theoretically it was possible that it was one shooter on the move, but the third shot had come from straight north, not northeast like the other two. There was a small group in action.

"You okay, honey?" she asked, her body shielded by the car in front of her.

"Yeah, but that was too close. We have to zero in on them."

Everyone ducked when another shot was heard, but nobody heard the whine of the bullet. For the next forty minutes, the squad would try to change position, but shots would come in, mostly aimed at

THE WORLD HUNGERS

Blake's un-reachable position under the truck. Sandra kept trying to keep the ladies under cover, but she was almost eaten alive by worry. Every shot at Blake was a shot at her soul. Whoever was out there had them pinned down, and she thanked God that the gunmen weren't too good at what they were doing, or else Blake would be dead already.

The mistake had been not having a forward observer of some sort, or not leaving a squad member to stay behind to watch the back trail for them. They never would have driven into the trap, and they wouldn't be pinned down. Part of the problem was that the ladies from the squad were literally two days freed from the slavers, and they only had theoretical training on the basics of the basics. They were raw recruits…but none of them were ready to give up, and all of them had the gleam of battle and fight in their souls. Every single one of them recognized the significance of the snipers trying to pick off Blake and Blake alone.

"Martha, keep everyone's heads down," Sandra whispered.

"What are you going to do?"

"Fix things. It's getting dark," she told Martha, who just nodded.

"I love you, Blake."

"Hurry back," he whispered, his body going numb from holding his position under the truck for so long.

"I'll try." And she was gone in the deepening shadows.

BOYD CRAVEN

They watched as Sandra faded into the darkening shadows of the late afternoon. The chickens made soft clucking sounds in the trailer above and behind Blake's position as he tried to keep an eye on everything out there. Lisa stuck close to Blake so she could watch after her "other" son, as she had started to think of him. She had marveled at how seamlessly her new life and family fit together, and she didn't want anything to break it up.

"I think I see her." Lisa pointed with her fingers to some swaying brush.

They all watched and waited.

§ § §

Sandra moved through the tall grass of the north side of the highway until she could ghost her way into the tree line. She was moving low to the ground, going from shadow to shadow. Her small form barely parted the grass or pushed a branch out of the way. She kept her senses focused on the area where the last shot had come from, and her entire body was as taut as piano wire from her concentration. She'd left the scoped rifle, instead carrying the M4 and her pistol. She kept the M4 ready as she moved as quickly and quietly as she could.

The shots had been fired from a distance, much further than any amateur had a right to try to take. The fact they were coming so close told her two things. That either the shots were meant to keep Blake and the ladies under cover as a delaying tactic, or that the shooters were good, just not as good as they thought. She hoped it was the latter, and not that there was another group of folks working themselves behind their group.

Her whole body went on high alert as she slowed her pace into the area where the shooting had come from. She crawled, going from cover to cover as she checked out the area. No shots or movements alerted her, and she was almost ready to move on to the next position where the shots were when she got a whiff of a coppery scent. Her heart dropped, but she kept going.

She found a hide. The ground had been kicked clean and clear by boots, and a camo net held up by four short lengths of rope was tied to some saplings. The view the shooter had would be easy pickings on the group if that'd been his intention. There were 30/.06 casings in the loose soil next to where an indentation the shape of a body had been pressed into the earth. All of this was disturbing enough, but what really scared her was the gut pile and the drag marks.

At first she didn't comprehend what she was seeing. She knelt down to get a better look and found a broken arrow shaft in the mess of guts. She picked it up with her fingertips, noting that the hunting broad head had been removed. Un-nerved, she dropped it and checked the woods all around her. She heard a twang and dropped just as an arrow hit her pack on the right side. Luckily it stopped without going all the way through.

BOYD CRAVEN

Sandra didn't see who had shot the arrow, but she fired two three-round bursts in that direction and heard more than one pair of running footsteps. She slid out of her pack and set herself behind a tree to keep the footsteps between the tree and her until she could make out that they were running away, deeper into the woods.

Her heart was pounding in her ears, and she had to concentrate on all of her surroundings and not have a terminal case of tunnel vision. She'd never been hunted before, and she had a sickening idea of what, if not who, the gut pile belonged to. She pulled the arrow from her pack, discarding the two tins of food that had stopped its progress and repacked everything.

"Do you need help?" Martha's voice crackled out of the radio she wore, breaking the silence.

"No, stay put. I'll check in every twenty minutes. Don't let anything or anyone come close. Something isn't right," Sandra whispered.

"Be careful." Her words were quiet and then the radio fell silent.

"I will," she whispered to the air, already putting her radio up.

Screams shattered the night, and she got to her feet, grabbed her rifle, and headed back towards the tree line to get a good look at where the sound was coming from. For half a heartbeat she feared it was her group, but the screams were male and coming from the wrong direction. She noted a tall syca-more tree to keep as a visual aid and noticed it was

THE WORLD HUNGERS

the same direction as some of the shots. She had a pretty good idea of what she was going to find, or not find, and she had to move almost three hundred yards through the woods to get there.

Maybe I should just go back and wait…No, I have to know if it's safe for us to move out, she thought to herself.

Again, she could smell the hide before she found it. The scent of blood and voided bowels hung heavy in the air, and she felt the hairs on her arms and neck come to attention as the goose bumps covered her flesh. Blood splashed around the clearing as if they hadn't gotten in a clean kill shot, and this time there wasn't a pile of guts, just brass casings from the shooter and a military-style framed backpack. That sent chills down her spine, and she edged into the camp, noting a similar setup as the hide before this one. The ground had been scraped clean, a camo netting was placed over the top…

"What are these guys doing? Who is hunting them down?"

This was the second time she was too late for answers, and she was almost afraid of skipping out on what she thought may have been a third position, but it was only a hundred yards away. Using the sycamore as a waypoint, she crawled over and found a half-gutted man and his equipment. A black arrow was sticking out of the side of his neck, low to the shoulder. The corpse had been stripped, and a cut started at his chest and traveled straight down to his groin. Her heart was beating hard, and the darkness of the night and the fact that somebody was hunting the hunters sent chills down her spine.

She'd endured live fire while overseas, had fought in more fights than the American public would have believed, and although she was a mechanic by trade, she was a soldier first and foremost. That being said, she was un-nerved and wanted Blake up here to get his take on things. She was fairly certain that there was one shooter for these last two hides, but she wasn't for sure. She pulled her radio out.

"Martha, Sandra here."

"Sandra, I read you."

"Get my husband, please."

"Is it safe? We heard the screams…"

"It's all right. He can come out now, I think."

She heard some rustling on the other end of the radio before the sounds cut off. When it clicked back on, her husband's voice made her smile slightly.

"Hey babe. Is everything fine up there?"

"The shooters are dead, but there's someone else out here."

"Should we move to cover?"

"Just…stay out of bow range."

"Bow range?"

"Can you ask Lisa and Martha to sit tight on the ladies and come up here with me? There's something I have to show you."

"Sure. They heard you and nodded. What is it?"

THE WORLD HUNGERS

"I'd rather not say out loud. See the sycamore tree about two o'clock from our position?"

"Yeah."

"Meet me under the tree, and Blake?"

"Yes?"

"Be careful. And prepare yourself. I'm kind of… unsettled up here."

§ § §

Blake met her under the tree. He got one look at her pale skin tone and hurried to her to check her for wounds. She slapped his hands away and pointed. He followed her gaze and her outstretched finger and almost missed the hide, it blended in so well. He took off at an easy gait that was the trademark of the former hermit. She wanted to yell to him to move from cover to cover, but he was already there before she could speak aloud. He took in the gory scene and then looked all around him.

"They had to have worked fast. How far away were you?"

"I can show you. Maybe two to three minutes."

"What was it like over there?"

"Somebody shot this at me. Hit my pack." She held up the black arrow.

"Somebody…" He looked at the arrow in his hand, one of the broad head blades snapped in half, and then to the arrow sticking out of the corpse's body. "Somebody is hunting people."

"That's what I thought. The first site has more

signs. I think there are tracks."

"Let's scavenge what we can from here, and then we'll head to that one. Is there more?"

"Yes, but I think this guy was using two spots."

"Makes sense. Kept us pinned down."

"I'm worried it may have been a delaying tactic. I'd like to show you this next spot and head back to the homestead as fast as we can."

"Let me get a look at all of this first before it gets completely dark. Then we can go."

CHAPTER 7

LEAVING ANN ARBOR

Neal and Patty had been fleeing by foot for days now. They traveled at night and avoided contact with everyone. Fleeing the large city hadn't been easy, and they were almost caught as they crossed the road a mile away from the apartment. They'd hid in a wooded area surrounding the tracks until the group had passed and then quietly slipped out the other way. One thing Neal commented on repeatedly was that walking was so much slower than riding his bike.

It took them two days of travel to reach the area where Bob usually stepped out. Neal tried calling for him quietly, but he never came. After hours of searching, they found a tar paper shack made out of saplings and old pallets alongside a crude outhouse. The smell coming out of both structures was horrid, but they felt that they had to at least look in the shack. Neal held his breath and poked his head inside the open doorway to look within the twelve-foot by twelve-foot structure.

Bob's corpse was laid out on an old army cot, his arm hanging off the edge. Something had gnawed at his fingertips, exposing the flesh underneath the skin, but despite that, Bob looked at piece. In one hand he held an envelope. Neal hesitated a moment too long getting in there, and Patty snuck by and looked.

"Is this your friend Bob?" she asked him, trying not to breathe through her nose.

"Yeah," he said softly.

"Look, here's an envelope. It's got your name on it, but it's spelled wrong."

"I never told him I spelled my name differently. It's probably for me."

She pulled it out of his fingers without touching the body and handed it to Neal. They both backed out of the shack, and he opened the heavy envelope. It contained a well-worn map that had been marked and laminated with clear contact paper. Inside the map were two folded pieces of notebook paper. The first one was addressed to him.

Neal, my heart has been bugging me and I'm writing this to tell you that my 20 years in seclusion is probably coming to an end. I joked with you once that I was never home-less, and I have many homes. Humble struc-

THE WORLD HUNGERS

tures, but I have them all over the country. My fall and winter homes are marked on the map. Reason I'm writing this, is I see in you a kindred spirit. Someone who doesn't like to live life with the noise and stress that others deal with.

I don't like people, I doubt you like them either. So I'm leaving all my worldly possessions to you, my last living friend. If you run across any of the old hobo crew and they question you, show them this note.

PS, I'm leaving you a list. It has what I can think of at each shelter. If you take your bike, you should be able to reach any of them within a day's travel, I know I could. My bones are getting too old to jump trains anymore.

- Bob

Neal read the note and handed it to Patty. He looked over the list. It had about twenty locations marked by a number. He opened the map to find it showed the railroads, many of the lines now unused. Highlighter marks under the lamination showed the routes Bob had traveled, and a black sharpie was used to mark off the number that correlated with the list.

"He mentioned a bike," Patty said, smiling.

"He did. Let's go look."

Behind the outhouse, they found not only one bike, but two. The first was an old Schwinn, and the second was a beat-up mountain bike of no name. Both of them were coated in a light layer of rust, and the chains barely turned. Neal knelt down and took off his pack. He got out the cooking spray that Patty had packed. He sprayed the chains down, and soon they were turning smoothly. Surprisingly, both bikes had decent pressure in the tires.

"What do you think?" Neal asked her.

"I don't know. We're still too close to Ann Arbor for my liking."

"Me too. I think all large cities are going to be death traps for a while."

"Do you want to camp here?" Patty asked, noticing the rising sun.

"Uh, not exactly here. Let's go down the tracks a bit."

"That's what I was hoping you'd say," she wrinkled her nose.

"I didn't see a shovel," Neal noted. "Sorry, Bob."

They were both pushing the bikes and their packs along the trail back towards the rail line when Neal stopped and pointed.

"Hey, look." He rubbed his finger across two brass tacks.

"Ohhh, hey, they're on the other side too."

"What do you think they are for?" he asked Patty.

"Markers?"

"You're probably right. Ready to find a place to camp?"

"Sounds good to me."

THE WORLD HUNGERS

§ § §

They traveled the railways, avoiding people. They stopped outside of Toledo the first night, literally chancing across the marker. Again, it was two push pins on the rail side and two pins pointing towards the shelter. It was another tarpaper shack, but this one was in better shape than the final resting place of Bob. It had seen much less use, and still had some provisions stocked up in it. Since they had fled without a lot of food, they had been living on short rations. Finding two five-gallon buckets in the corner almost had them smiling. The buckets were still sealed tight, and Neal pried one lid off and found a treasure trove.

Matches, fishing line with hooks, can opener, plastic bags, a tarp, utensils, and some rope. The other bucket almost made them weak in the knees when they opened it. They pulled out cheap dollar bags of rice, beans, and lentils, and half a dozen cans of beef stew underneath that. Patty took one look at Neal, who almost never showed emotion, and she saw a small smile touching the corner of his mouth. She threw him a can. Soon both of them were eating directly out of the opened cans. The rich food hit their stomachs and they immediately began to feel drowsy.

"We have to do something about water," Neal told her, holding up an almost empty plastic pop bottle.

"Yeah. There's some fishing line, so we should

be able to find water close by."

They fell into a heavy sleep, each of them sitting up across from each other. It had been the first good rest since they had left Ann Arbor. When they woke up, it was still light outside, but night was falling fast. They stretched and went looking around, listening for anything.

"I wonder if he has an outhouse here," Patty said, pulling her hair back into a ponytail.

"If not, I need to find a tree to kill," Neal told her with a deadpan expression.

"You're so gross."

"I was kidding," he said, trying to make light of the situation.

"Oh hey, there's two little buildings back here."

There was another crude outhouse, but it became obvious that this one was in better shape, or had less use. Neal let Patty go first and approached the second structure. It was another pallet and tarpaper construction, but it lacked any sort of doorway or windows. He walked in and found an old galvanized pail and an old fishing rod. The fiberglass had spider web cracks, and the old spinning reel was pitted with rust. Skeptically, Neal picked it up and shook it, fully expecting it to snap on him. To his surprise, it didn't. The door of the outhouse opened and Patty joined him.

"Your turn," she said, bumping him with her shoulder.

"Just a sec," he mumbled, looking around.

"What?"

THE WORLD HUNGERS

"This little building. What was it for?"

"I don't know. A shed?"

They looked around, but nothing else stuck out to them. Neal used the outhouse, pleasantly surprised that there were 3 rolls of toilet paper that were relatively free from rodent damage and water. When he was done, he looked around and found Patty back at the first shack, playing with a coffee can.

"What are you doing?"

"Starting a small fire."

"How come? And why the can?"

"It's a hobo heater," she said, then she looked up at him and snorted out a laugh. "That wasn't deliberate; it's probably what Bob used to cook with."

"Really?"

"Yeah, they're easy and cheap to make. Take a big metal coffee can or something and cut a hole in the side to fit a soup can. Cut both sides off the soup can and shove that in the hole. Then put dry sticks inside the can. Put your skillet or pot over top of the little stove and voila."

"That looks too easy."

"It is. I had a commercial version of this with my camping gear, but I didn't have room to pack it. It takes about half a dozen pencil-sized sticks to boil water."

"Does that mean…?"

"Coffee." Patty smiled as she started to dig through her pack.

Neal wandered off to gather fuel, his thoughts

spinning faster than he could articulate. He knew they couldn't stay in this location forever, but they were tired and had gone without rest. They also had no particular place to go, so as long as they were safe, they might as well be somewhere. He realized that staying up in the northern climates was a no-win situation for him, not with the cities seemingly in chaos. Their hope lay south. They had to find some place where they could avoid winter and start over.

One more thing he had to ponder was Patty. She was pretty, kind, and for the first time in his life, he felt comfortable with her presence. What he didn't feel though was the smitten feeling. It wasn't as if cupid had shot him with an arrow thing. He wasn't sure how she felt either, and he didn't feel capable of asking her about it. Little hints suggested to him that she was at least fond of him, such as the shoulder bump, the hugs, and the kiss on the cheek. But he didn't want to push her away just because he didn't have feelings for her, not like that. Neal also didn't want to be alone anymore. Now that he'd had a taste of friendship, he was cautiously optimistic that this new world may push him into situations that formerly would have overloaded his spinning mind. He would have to adapt, react, and survive. Dying because he was afraid to act wasn't an option. With that in mind, he brought an armload of sticks and twigs to the shack and dropped the pile by the doorway.

Patty smiled and started to break the twigs into

small eight- to ten-inch pieces. When she finished, she fished out one of the numerous lighters she had in her camping bag.

"Do you think we should stick around here for a while?" he asked, watching her pour the rest of her water into a small pan to boil.

"It's as good a place as any. Besides, we have to find water, especially if you want more than a second cup of coffee."

"Hey, I'll go use that metal bucket. I can almost smell the water close by. We can boil that or do the bleach trick."

"Sounds good. Hey, I've been meaning to ask… you grabbed that satchel off the Islamist. What was in it?"

Neal's face squinted together in thought, and then he walked out to the cargo rack on his bike and brought it back into the hut.

"I forgot about that." He tossed it to her. "It's probably just his school papers. We can always use it for tinder," he told her, then put his own bottle down before heading out to grab the galvanized bucket.

Finding the stream wasn't as hard as he thought, and he could smell the water. The problem was, he could smell it everywhere. As he got closer, he found an old pathway through the brush that led to a fast-flowing creek. Frogs croaked and launched themselves into the deeper, faster moving water, and cattails lined the one shore. Neal scooped a big bucketful of water out from the middle where the current was the fastest, getting his legs wet, then lugged the heavy pail back to the shack. He walked in and Patty handed him a steel mug of coffee that she'd made from the single packs of instant coffee she'd had in her camping gear.

Her face was blank, and she looked up at Neal after a long moment of silence.

"This is bad." She was holding a manila folder containing some papers and color photos.

"What is it?"

"Plans. On how…" she choked up. "How to destroy our country. Before the invasion."

"Invasion?"

CHAPTER 8

KENTUCKY

"They've been gone a long time," Lisa told the group.

"I think we should at least get things ready for us to roll. What do you ladies think?" Martha asked everyone.

"A couple of us should stand guard on the trucks and animals," Corinne, one of the squad's young ladies, commented.

"That sounds good. Pick somebody to help, and the rest of us can go and see if we can push these cars out of the way."

"Lisa, want to stick back with me while the others go move those cars?"

"Sure. Do you think it's safe?"

"You heard Sandra. She found something, but I don't think there's any more danger down here. If we need to go in a hurry…"

"We're still blocked in," Karen, a fiery redhead in her early twenties said.

"So let's do something about it, squad." Martha said, a little tingle of excitement working its way up her body.

Corinne and Lisa stuck back to watch the supplies, and the rest of the group, led by Martha and Karen, cautiously approached the road block. Both cars had keys in their ignitions, and the shifters were already in neutral. It took four of them to rock the first car enough to push it towards the shoulder, where the slope and gravity finally took it over and it rolled into the tall grass. The second car's wheels were turned, and it wouldn't move as easily. It took both Karen and Martha to turn the steering wheel straight so they could push it back. Again, with everyone helping, it wasn't that difficult once they got the car rolling.

The ladies gave each other high fives. Wiping the sweat from their foreheads, they started back to the trucks. They got into position to cover all points of the compass again, and Martha was about to key the radio and check on Sandra when Blake's voice came out of the unit.

"We're coming out. Don't shoot."

"I hear you. See you soon."

They waited several minutes until Lisa spotted Blake's form stepping out of the tree line, followed by Sandra. They were hurrying, not trying to run crouched down, just running. It wasn't an all-out panic sprint, but everyone tensed as they watched them, their rifles pointed and ready to defend them from whatever they were running from. Blake especially was having a hard time. He was carrying a large pack that he hadn't gone into the woods with.

"I wonder where he got that?" Lisa asked no one in particular.

"What are they running from?" Karen asked.

"I don't know, but look sharp. If it's bad enough to spook Blake and Sandra, it has to be bad."

"I'll go fire up one of the trucks. Let's get everything staged to roll."

"Mount up ladies," Martha shouted.

The squad got in the trucks, leaving the passenger doors open. Sandra and Blake jumped into separate pickups, and neither objected when the trucks took off.

"How bad was it, Blake?" Lisa asked.

"As bad as it gets. Do you want me to drive?"

"When we get to the lane. It's been over twenty years since I drove a stick shift."

"You seem to be doing alright." He grinned.

"Fear is a great motivator."

"True that."

§ § §

Duncan got one look at his daughter and Blake's expressions and called a mini meeting in the main house. The squad planned to unload the loot at a later time. Lisa just nodded, and Martha sent Karen to go fetch Chris and the Cayhill boys from the barn.

"What's gotten you so shaken up?" Duncan asked his daughter. Sandra just pinched her lips together and shook her head. She grabbed a large box of medications from the bed of the pickup truck and carried it in.

"Blake, what is it?"

He gave the preacher a long look.

"We better wait for everyone who's coming to sit in."

"It's bad?"

"It's abomination," he told Duncan. Blake grabbed a load of supplies and disappeared into the house as well.

Duncan stood there, dazed at the raw fear and emotion coming out of the two of them, and noticed that no one else there was affected the same way.

"It must be," he muttered before grabbing a box himself and heading in.

Before he could set his box down, he heard retching noises in the bathroom. Worried, he headed over to check it out.

"You can't know that for sure." His daughter's voice stopped his outstretched hand from knocking.

"Why else would they dress him out?" His words were replaced with more wet sounds, and Duncan stepped away from the door, rocked.

"Wipe your face," he heard his daughter say before he stepped into the kitchen to look for something.

"What are you looking for?" Lisa asked Duncan, putting her arms around his chest and hugging him from behind.

"Something."

"Well, yeah, what kind of something?"

"I don't know. Do you know what this is about?"

"No, Blake refused to talk about it. It's got him scared, scared badly."

"Is that him throwing up?"

"I think so."

The bathroom door opened, and a pale Blake stepped out, followed by Sandra. He wiped the sweat off his brow and sat at the kitchen table. Soon, the rest of the core of the homestead was there, waiting for Blake to speak. Sandra kept rubbing his hand and arm, and everyone could almost feel the waves of unease radiating from the solitary man.

"We were ambushed on the way back to the homestead. None of us were hurt, and Sandra went out there to scare off or neutralize the threat. There were some complications, and she called me on the radio and asked me to come up and look things over." He took a sip of water and waited for his wife to go on.

"I called Blake up to the north side of the highway where the shooters had been," she said, rolling a black shafted arrow in her hand. "I found a sniper hide. The shooter was gone. Mostly. I found a broken arrow like this one, in a pile of guts."

Everyone blanched at that.

"Was it an animal kill?" Bobby asked.

"No, I don't think so. I think that was what was left of the shooter," Blake told them.

"Somebody took a shot at me with this arrow." Sandra held it up. "My pack killed the momentum and it didn't hit me, just ruined some canned goods. But there was more than one person who was hunting out there. I fired in the direction the arrow came from and I could hear running footsteps."

"Carbon hunting arrow." Weston held it up so he could see it better.

"Yeah. When I felt it was safe, I checked around and found a second and third sniping spot. I'd obviously disrupted something, because the body was still there."

"They didn't have time to finish gutting the body and carry away the carcass," Blake told them, looking sick again.

"What do you mean by carcass?"

"The other shooter. They hadn't had time to finish field dressing him out," Blake told them softly.

Everyone took an instinctive gulp and looked around.

"I told Blake that it doesn't mean that they were cannibals," Sandra made their fears heard aloud.

"That first gut pile told me all I needed to know. Especially how they were starting to dress the second shooter."

"What do you mean?" Duncan asked, his hand over the left side of his chest, massaging it.

THE WORLD HUNGERS

"The gut pile. The heart and liver weren't there. The second man was cut open from crotch to sternum. Everything else was in the gut pile, but they took the heart and liver along with the carcass."

Everyone looked a little green.

"I didn't notice that." Sandra's voice was small and soft. She gave his hand a squeeze and looked up.

"From what we could tell, there were at least six to eight different boot prints we could make out."

"So we have six to eight sickos out there?" Duncan said.

"Not necessarily." Blake looked at him, sickened. "There were footprints all over. I don't know how many of them belonged to the snipers and how many belonged to the cannies," he said, making a nickname out of thin air.

"This is really serious," Lisa said. "First we had snipers waiting for us, and now cannibals? Hunting us?"

"It looks like it to me."

"I can't even begin to tell you how wrong this is," Duncan said. "We're going to have to keep working with the squad, and everyone else who can shoot. That way—"

"If we're ever attacked in massive numbers, we can defend ourselves," Sandra finished for him.

"Some of the ladies are comfortable around me. I'll work with any of them or the families who are willing," Weston said from where he leaned up against the counter, his expression neutral.

"I'll do what I can," Bobby piped in, but like Duncan, he was still on restricted duty.

"Do we have enough scraps to start making more toe tappers?" Sandra asked.

"No, not really."

"Ok, so new rule. Nobody goes out unarmed." Blake said, standing up and rubbing his stomach.

"Except the kids?" Sandra asked, watching little Chris play with some toy cars they found in the barn in the open doorway of the other room.

"Well, I'd like to see the ten- to twelve-year-olds know how to handle and shoot, if only to keep them from finding something and getting hurt if they don't know any better. If they can defend themselves…" Blake said.

"Let's get the rest of the supplies unloaded, and then we'll all cook a big meal and discuss things," Weston said, pushing away from the counter and standing next to Blake.

The group broke up, and Blake went in to see Chris. The boy was all smiles.

"Hey Dad, want to play with these cars? We found some in boxes in the barn."

"You know what? I'd love to play cars with you." He lay down on the floor in front of Chris, his heart almost bursting with love.

Sandra stood in the doorway a moment, watching her men. Then she headed off to find Lisa. Her wedding had been rushed because she never knew what the next day would bring, and she wanted to make sure that Lisa and her father were afforded the

THE WORLD HUNGERS

same opportunities. She heard Lisa's voice coming from the basement, so she headed down. She was on the bottom rung of the stairs when she stopped dead.

Duncan was down on one knee.

"I never know what's going to happen anymore. One thing I am for sure about, is my love for you. Times are getting more and more frightening, and I don't want to miss out on a life with you. Lisa Cahill, will you marry me?"

"Yes, you big fool. I love you too." Lisa's smile was beaming, and her skin had flushed an alarming red.

She wiped her eyes and looked up, seeing Sandra standing in the doorway.

"Congratulations," Sandra squeaked and ran back upstairs, forgetting what she had come down for.

CHAPTER 9

TRAVELING FROM ANN ARBOR

J ust dangle the hook in front of his mouth," Patty whispered from the side of the shore.

They hadn't trusted the old fishing pole enough to lose some line over it, so they improvised a cane pole from a long sturdy stick with the fishing line tied on. A bare hook finished off the ensemble, and they had taken it to the creek to try their luck. He had told Patty about the frogs he saw the last time, and her eyes had gone wide and she smiled.

Neal all but smacked the bull frog with the hook before it snapped its head almost faster than his eyes could track. The improvised rod almost jerked out of his hand when the frog leapt into the water and started swimming. At the last second, he kept his grip on it and pulled up, making the wood flex under the weight of the frog. He swung it over to

THE WORLD HUNGERS

the shore by Patty, holding it up at eye level to her.

"Now what?"

She took it off, put it in the metal bucket, and sat across the open top. She motioned to the creek. "You keep fishing."

They spent the whole afternoon like that, and when they had a dozen croakers in the bucket, they went back to the camp. A fillet knife to the head ended the frogs quickly and humanely. Patty cut off the hind legs, putting the rest of the frog into a pile by the outhouse.

"We can use parts of them for bait tomorrow."

Neal nodded and watched as she used a thin stick whittled into a needled point. She skewered the legs like shish kebobs and put them over the fire. Slowly they cooked, and she moved the stick constantly. The skin on the legs dried out, and as the meat cooked, it pulled away from the flesh and turned almost black. When the meat looked white, Patty took one leg off the end and pulled the skin back. She broke off a piece of the meat and looked at it.

"Looks good," she told him. She started to chew on it like a chicken wing.

Neal had never tried frog, but he was hungry and it smelled good. He was having a hard time believing that he was about to eat something that he'd caught, something he watched get killed. His stomach almost rebelled, but the gnawing hunger inside of him made it a small, almost inconsequential matter. He followed suit and was surprised that

101

the flesh tasted almost like chicken in its neutral texture and flavor. It was done in a moment, and he put the bones neatly across the ones that Patty had laid down by the fire.

"Needs salt," he told her, deadpan.

"You just ate a frog, and all you can say is it needs salt?"

"Ribbit ribbit?" he said.

"Neal, I'm going to get you," she told him, a mischievous grin on her face as she set the skewer down.

Neal looked up, startled. He was expecting anger but couldn't process what she was doing. She stalked to his side of the shack, a smile on her face. In three quick steps she was there, almost tackling him, her fingers tickling at his side. He let out a surprised laugh and scooted back until his backside hit the pallets.

"It needs salt?"

Patty was straddling his legs, pinning him in place.

"It wasn't bad. I kind of liked it, it just needed salt."

Neal's heart was racing, and not from excitement. Fear. Suddenly uncomfortable and backed into the wall, he felt helpless, vulnerable. He turned his head and tried to grab her waist to push her back when she suddenly kissed him. His whole body stiffened and he held still, letting her, waiting for it to be over. Patty pushed herself back after a few moments, a hurt look on her face.

THE WORLD HUNGERS

"I'm sorry Neal. I forgot, and I figured…" she made her way to her feet and went to the other side of the hobo stove and looked away.

"Do you have any pepper then?" he asked her.

"Pepper? Pepper?" The last was almost a shriek.

"I was of course, trying to joke," he told her softly as he stood. "I'm sorry, I just don't feel the same way about things." With that said, he headed out to the bike.

He sat down on the ground, pulling his knees to his stomach and circling his arms around them. He rocked for a while, his mind whirling. He'd known that this could happen, and now his own nature had hurt the one person left in this world that mattered to him. He felt the pain in his chest at that thought and then had to stop and wonder. Pain, he felt it. It wasn't physical, it was more emotional. He considered that some more. It was starting to get dark, and they had abandoned the nocturnal lifestyle a week back for convenience. He was deep into his mind, exploring his feelings when he felt Patty drop down beside him and pull him close to her with one arm.

"I'm sorry Patty," he told her quietly.

"No, it isn't you who should be sorry. I'm not being fair to you. I just got so caught up in the moment…"

"Patty, other than my mom, you're the only girl that I've ever been comfortable around. You're my best friend and I don't want to lose that."

"You won't. I'll try not to make you uncomfortable. Will you come back inside with me and finish dinner?"

"Sure, just give me a couple minutes. I'm sorting things out," he told her.

She nodded and left. Lately he'd said that phrase a lot. *I'm sorting things out.* She'd come to understand that Neal's mind wasn't adapting to the change in the world as well as some people were able to, and it was his way of coping. In truth, Neal was fighting his own anxieties, insecurities, and feelings. He could compartmentalize all day long, but at some point, he needed to sit down and analyze things in his own mind. She got that, and so she left him to sort things out. He tried to focus on his feelings, the pain. Instead, the documents from the Islamist kept coming back into his head.

It detailed a broad, reaching plan that had been ongoing for the last twenty years. Sleepers were sent in and told to wait until a good opportunity presented itself. Of course, it hadn't for twenty years, and only some of them had been activated for random acts or espionage. The easiest way they were able to infiltrate was through the student visa program. Another popular method was to come across one of the borders. Drug smugglers had taken advantage of the open borders of the United States for decades, and illegal immigrants and Islamists had followed suit. From both the Mexican side and the Canadian side. The student that had died by Neal's hands had been a recent immigrant and had come knowing the end game was upon them.

He was assigned it ignite Ann Arbor's Muslim

THE WORLD HUNGERS

population to rise up. They knew that even non-believers would rise up, as evidenced by Ferguson, Missouri, the Rodney King riots in LA, and even Detroit back in the sixties. Small race fights and protests had peppered American history for the last hundred years. The general plan was to destabilize the major population centers and allow the American culture to implode upon itself. They estimated that simply taking the power out would cause a ninety percent mortality to the general population in the first month. Three weeks to a month later would knock out another one to two percent as supplies ran out. Sickness and violence would take out all but one percent of the population after a year.

The numbers were painted using a broad brush, but it was terrifying. In the two weeks that they'd stayed in Ann Arbor, they'd witnessed the way things were breaking down, had seen the fires in the distance. Patty had heard rumors that large gangs roamed freely, preaching the convert or die mantra. They'd avoided that as long as they could, and when attacked, they fled. Only by hiding and using the railways were they able to avoid people. Time was getting fuzzy for Neal, but he knew that they were approaching the one month mark, more or less. They'd survived better than ninety percent, but it was what was to happen in the third month that he was worried about.

The plans were vague, and probably because the Islamist carrying it was only a mid-level stooge, but it outlined an invasion force. It would start on both coasts, capturing strategic assets. Those who lived in the Midwest and heartlands were to link up with those forces after causing as much havoc and destruction as they could.

Neal saw the plan for what it was—a brilliant but ugly way to win a war with a super power without causing a lot of loss for the opposition. The first part was already accomplished, and Neal wondered what would happen once the invaders came. He wondered what the state of the military overseas was, or the Navy, who had technology that was hardened off from the effects of an EMP. He kept trying to refocus his attention on his almost break-through on his feelings, but he soon gave up. He would just have to be careful around Patty for now, to make sure he didn't hurt her or her feelings.

He stood, and his joints popped. He stretched to get the cold out of his bones, and his stomach rumbled at the smell of food. Neal marveled at how hunger made almost everything smell wonderful. He headed back into the shack, sat down across from her, and took his half of the skewer, eating quickly. Once or twice their eyes met, but neither of them were ready to deal with it more.

"When do you think we should leave?" Patty asked after a while.

"I don't know. Food here is almost gone. We can live on frogs and fish for a while, but I don't even know where to go."

"I've been thinking about that a little bit," she

told him, finishing off her last piece. "If the invasion is going to happen on either coast, wouldn't it make sense to move to the center of the country, the heartlands, as the Islamists called it?"

"Sure. Any place in mind?"

"It would have to be somewhere that we could survive the winters easily, lots of food or game."

"I don't know how to hunt or trap," he told her, knowing it sounded dumb.

"I know how to do small game. Something larger like a deer wouldn't be that bad."

"We don't have all that much ammo."

"I know, but if we avoid people and can survive the worst of the—"

Rapid gunfire startled them into silence, and screams filled the night. They hurriedly knocked the top off the hobo stove and stomped on the embers. They scooped dirt from the floor onto the embers and started packing their supplies, not knowing how long they had. In truth, they had discussed this a couple days back. At the first sign of problems, they would melt off into the distance, following the tracks. The gunfire could be close, or the sound could be coming from a long ways off, but the shouting had to be close.

It took them ten minutes to clear camp. They took everything, right down to the metal bucket that they strapped to the back of Neal's backpack, and headed into the darkening night.

"I was hoping for one more night on that cot," Neal griped.

"Yeah, we'll have to find some place up ahead. You'll have to sleep under the tarp with me."

"As long as you don't try to tickle me again."

"Oh, it was the tickling that bugged you?" Despite the situation, she was grinning, her legs pumping the pedals hard.

"Let's hurry. I don't think they knew we were there," he told her, but a rare smile tugged the corners of his mouth.

They rode for another hour before they slowed down to look for a spot, but the sound of a distant shot kept them riding again. They passed through small towns, the silent speed of their bikes allowing them to move through the gloom unmolested. Finally, when dawn was starting to tug at the edges of the skyline, they stopped.

"I'm exhausted," Neal admitted.

"Let's get a drink and…"

Neal was already pushing his bike off the railway towards the weeds. He dropped his pack and rolled it over until he found a soft spot, then laid his head and shoulders on it. Patty joined him, pulling out a green tarp weighted down on one end. She pulled it over her like a blanket and curled into Neal. He fell asleep listening to her soft snores, her breathing coming in a steady rhythm.

CHAPTER 10

THE HOMESTEAD, KENTUCKY

Do you, Father, or Pastor Duncan to the rest of ya, take Lisa to be your lawfully wedded wife?" Sandra asked.

"I do." Duncan was beet red.

"And Lisa, do you take my father to be your lawfully wedded husband, and agree to be my mother and grandmother of Chris?"

"I do." She smiled.

"By the power vested in me, which only comes from God since the power went out and the world as we knew it ended, I now pronounce you man and wife. Welcome to the family Lisa, and Daddy, you may now—"

She was cut off by Duncan, who waved a hand at her for fooling around. He was already wrapping his arms around Lisa and kissing her. He didn't stop, and soon the kiss deepened and the entire homestead cheered. Soon, the feast was on, and without instruments to play, everyone sang songs and danced as they felt like it. As far as weddings went, this one was unconventional, but it was probably something that people had done long before there was written law and ceremonies revolving around licenses and witnesses signing a piece of paper.

Bobby and Weston had cleaned the camper the previous day, and that's where Lisa and Duncan retired when it got dark. Blake joked that he'd put in enough provisions to last a few days, to poke at the preacher for doing the same with him, but Lisa surprised them all and said a few days may not be enough. Blake's cheeks burned crimson and Sandra laughed and laughed. Bobby set out to his spot along the lane to watch for incoming foot traffic and lights, and Weston headed to the dorms.

Nobody enjoyed going through the old well and the tunnel very much, but it kept the appearance that the barn was exactly what it was and not a house to tons of people. Everyone else turned in, and except for Melissa sneaking out to be with Bobby, the homestead slept off the rich food and fun of the wedding day.

§ § §

"Blake, there's something I wanted to talk to you about," Sandra rolled over, pressing her body against her husband's and pulling the covers over

THE WORLD HUNGERS

their nude forms.

"Yeah hon?"

"What should we do about those hunters?"

"Hunters? You mean the cannibals?"

"Yeah," Sandra said, the thought making her body ripple with a shiver.

"I don't know. We need to learn more about them, find out how many there are."

"Make sure they aren't a threat to the homestead here?"

"Yeah. I'm worried about sending us all out like we took out the slavers. I don't want another group to attack us while we're gone. We'd lose everything."

"Yeah, we can't do things like that anymore."

"What if I took Weston, and we checked things out for a while?"

"Why wouldn't you take me?"

"Because, you're my GI Jane, and somebody needs to be in charge of our homestead security. Besides, you're training your squad."

"I am," Sandra said, chewing on her lip in thought. "Are you sure it isn't because…"

"I'm smarter than that. You are more than capable of going. Only reason I'm suggesting me is that Dad and Lis…er…Mom are busy, Bobby is still recovering, and I don't know the rest of the group enough to know who knows what. Most of them were pretty traumatized. I think if I could go with Weston, you and the rest can more than keep the homestead safe."

"Two people draw less attention…" Sandra said,

her voice uncertain.

"Yes, especially if we go on foot and treat this like a hunting expedition."

"Will you be gone long?"

"I hope not. Maybe a day to hike to where you were attacked and a day to watch. Depending on what we can find, maybe more."

"Three to four days?" She buried her head under his chin, tears wetting his chest.

"I don't know what else to do," he whispered.

"Me neither. It just seems like there are threats all around us, nonstop. That's why I got out of the army. I didn't want to look over my shoulder every five minutes."

"I know, baby."

"Speaking of babies…"

"Wait, you're pregnant?"

"No, but we have to work on that." Her tear-streaked face was smiling, he could feel it.

"Good deal."

§ § §

Blake talked to Weston about a scouting trip, and the former cop agreed immediately. It'd been in Weston's thoughts for the last couple of days. They debated waiting for Duncan and Lisa to come back from their honeymoon, but neither of them thought they could afford to wait. It'd already been two days, and they were afraid of not being able to backtrack. They both elected to take an M4. Blake took one that Duncan had been playing with that had a scope on it.

In some of the now sorted equipment they took from the slavers, Duncan found a suppressor and many fun goodies to trick out the M4s. It was Duncan's baby that he'd taken to the field with him. Lightweight and with a decent range, it left him room to carry enough ammo for a sustained firefight. The less they carried, the less weighted down they would be. Food would be some of the dried goods and very few of the jarred or canned goods. The exception was good old Spam.

They were going to have cold camps overnight, so they both took small tarps and a sleeping bag and crammed them into framed packs. Blake and Weston checked each other over for anything loose. Both carried side arms and a knife, and when they felt good, they headed off down the lane, their camouflaged forms eventually melting into the lush green of the late summer woods.

"We have half a day before we get close to where we have to start sneaking in. Want to move fast, or take it easy going in?" Blake asked.

"Let's see how it goes. I'm not used to these hills the way you are. You'd probably walk me into the ground."

"Fair enough."

They were silent for a while, concentrating on their footing once they left the lane. The traveled west, putting the sun at their backs.

"Oh, this is great. Remind me to come back

here sometime soon," Blake told Weston, rubbing his hand on the trunk of a tree that was heavy with fruit that looked like blackberries.

"Is this a mulberry tree?"

"Yeah, black mulberry. It's a wonder the birds haven't found this one yet."

Weston picked a few and popped them in his mouth.

"Pretty good," he said.

"Yeah, there's a ton of wild food out here in the woods if you know what to look for."

"Point out some for me. The wild foods."

"No problem."

They walked in silence for a while longer, and Blake stopped, running his hands through some green buds on a plant.

"Common milkweed. I've eaten the green buds like these. You just soak them in cold water to float the bugs out, then you can steam them or use them like peas. The flowers are supposed to be good too, but I haven't tried them like that."

"Isn't milkweed poisonous?"

"Hasn't killed me. I used to collect a ton of this stuff when money was tight. Canned it mostly when I had too much."

They continued their walk, Blake pointing out little things here and there. They crossed a small stream and he showed him the cattails and explained how the roots could be dug up and baked like potatoes. There were other things that could be done with them, but Blake hadn't tried.

THE WORLD HUNGERS

"What about lily pads?"

"Never tried. It's illegal," he said and smiled at the former cop.

The talking petered out as the day lengthened. They started to slow, and spaced themselves out so they wouldn't make an easier target for snipers or the cannies that had hunted Sandra and the group who had set out to ambush them. They made it to the site of the butchering by nightfall, and the two days in the heat had made the offal almost unbearable to be near.

"They came back for the other body," Blake whispered as they approached the second site.

"The tracks look fresher here."

"Probably waited a day or so to come back out."

"Can you follow the tracks?"

"That's what we're here for."

The trail the cannies left wasn't hard to follow, but the light was getting bad. They ate a meal of flat bread and smoked venison under the cover of the heavy brush. After several uncomfortable hours, they fell asleep. Hours later a snapping twig woke Weston, who rolled over and nudged Blake through his sleeping bag.

"Shhhh, I heard something," Weston whispered to Blake, who almost startled awake.

Weston pointed. Another branch snapped nearby, and the sound of soft footsteps carried to them.

"Over here. Do you think it was her?"

"I don't know. If you hadn't botched the shot—"

"I wasn't trying to kill her outright."

"In the end, they all end up on Kenny's hooks, don't they?" A soft chuckle followed this.

Both Blake and Weston had buried their sleeping bags in fallen leaves from the previous autumn, and used pine boughs to hold things down. It made for a warm and camouflaged bed, but it was noisy and restrictive to their movements in this situation. They were literally caught with their pants down and vulnerable. Weston put his finger up to his lips and Blake nodded, feeling inside his bag for his pistol.

"I've never tried a kid. You think if we get a chance, we could...?"

"Be quiet, look. I see their tracks. They're somewhere around here."

Then things went silent. Both Blake and Weston were able to get their pistols and began slowly extracting themselves from the leaves as they heard the footsteps come and go of the hunters trying to figure out where the homestead men were hiding. Once in a while they would get close, but they moved off far enough that eventually both men were able to pull their pants up and slide out of their bags.

"I could only hear two of them," Blake said, breaking the silence.

"Definitely part of the group we want. What do you want to do?"

"Kill them all. Realistically, capture one, find out where they are?"

THE WORLD HUNGERS

"Should we do that, or just wait for them to leave the area and backtrack them?" Weston asked.

"That sounds like a safer bet," Blake replied.

"Do we stay hunkered down here, or risk moving?" Weston whispered.

"Let's get ready to move quick if we need to, but I'd rather not get into a big gunfight now that I've had a moment to think about it."

Weston just nodded in response, and they packed up their cold camp as quietly as they could, using the pine bough to brush out any sign they'd been there. Then they hid themselves.

"I know they are around here somewhere," a voice from the left sounded out.

"You know you saw their tracks. Maybe they came back and scouted around and left."

"You know Marv, maybe they are hunting us."

There was a long pause. Both men held their breaths.

"No, there's no better hunters than us, Jerry. I'd know if we were being hunted."

"Ok, well, let's circle around and see if we can pick up their trail again. Maybe backtrack them to their camp."

Their voices and footfalls faded as they moved off, and both Blake and Weston stood uneasily.

"They're going to backtrack us," Weston muttered.

"Back to the first plan?"

"Kill them all?"

"No, grab one for questioning. Kill the other,"

117

Blake replied.

"We have to get in front of them somehow. These guys are good."

"That's my take on it too. If they find our homestead…"

"Don't worry, we're armed for bear. From what I saw, the one guy had a crossbow and the other had a compound bow. Think they are out of ammo?" Weston asked.

"God, I hope so."

"Why?"

"Because if they are hunting with a bow and they still have ammo, they must be good, better than me more than likely."

"Thanks, Blake. You've just officially scared me silly."

"Well, let's go, Mr. Silly."

CHAPTER 11

KENTUCKY

Neal and Sandra had stayed at many of Bob's stops along the way, but when they found a remote shack in Kentucky that was better stocked than their earlier stops and had a wood stove, they decided to stay. There were three of the tarpaper buildings and an outhouse. One of the buildings was filled with firewood, the other with various tools and five-gallon buckets stacked against one wall.

"I wonder what his obsession is with the buckets?" Neal asked.

"Vermin and weather proof. Mostly," Patty answered him.

In some of the buckets, they found books. Patty raised an eyebrow at some of the titles, but Neal devoured the info on quiet nights. One of them was *Survival Poaching* by Ragnar Benson, another was *Mantrapping*. There were other books in there about wild plants and trapping animals. Loads and loads of fictional works were stored in the small twelve-by-twelve building.

"I think this was his winter camp?" Neal said.

"Looks like it. It'd have to be pretty remote for him to want to stay in one place long."

The main house/shack had an old bunk bed frame that had been strung with nylon ropes. They were surprised at how sturdy the bed was, and how comfortable it was when they lay on it. Almost like a hammock. The pallets on the inside of the structure had been stuffed with leaves and newspaper, then covered with the rough sawn boards of other pallets. The only touch of the modern world was the metal piece that the stove pipe went through; it was attached to the wall and went out through the side of the house. The rest of it could almost have come out of a *Boy's Life* magazine. There was even a rough table and stools made out of pallets and logs that had been turned up on the cut end.

They almost wept as they found other buckets with dried goods. Beans, rice, lentils. In one, they even found spices and cookware.

"Are you thinking what I'm thinking?" Neal asked her.

"Tickle time?" she threatened.

"No, that this is some place we could stay for a while. And maybe get the rest of this info to somebody in authority."

THE WORLD HUNGERS

"If there is somebody in authority."

§ § §

They spent the next two weeks resting and trying their hand with the supplies. A hand-drawn map in one bucket led them to the woods, where underneath an old stump that had been pushed over in a storm they found a fifty-gallon barrel that had metal traps in it, along with a setting tool. Neal recognized them as conibears. Traps that had been used in many of the books that he'd been reading at night.

Another wonder was that the stream was close by, so they didn't have to go far for water. Every location they stopped had water somewhere close by, according to Bob's maps. This one was deep, narrow, and had plenty of fish swimming through it. They knew that if they were going to survive the winter, they'd need to put in some sort of meat for the long term.

Using the books, Neal constructed a wooden teepee that was almost four feet across at the base, and six feet tall. He nailed saplings to the four corners for stability, and small pencil-sized branches across those to make a sort of grill. He weaved them together when he could, but it didn't turn out that well. Patty helped as much as she could, but she was amused by his sudden interest in learning this sort of thing, and mostly watched him. What he came up with was ugly, but practical. He hung a strand of paracord down and through the shelf with a metal hook on one end. He told Patty that it'd be where they could hang the pot they'd found in the shack. It was an old galvanized pot with a wire handle.

"So what are you going to do now?"

"Wrap it with canvas or your tarp, then catch some fish, trap some animals, and start smoking the meat."

She almost giggled at that, but soon was as caught up with the food storage as he was. They checked the traps daily to see if they had any luck. They'd use the offal of the carcasses as fishing bait during the time they weren't trapping, and they tried different methods for smoking. The best thing they found was to get a bed of embers going, or to make a campfire elsewhere and get a big bed of them ready and shovel them in the teepee. Then they'd take wood chips that had been soaked in water and put those across the top. Once in a while they'd have to add more wood or more embers, but with some trial and error they finally made a sort of smoked fish fillet jerky. They also found that although they stink when alive, groundhogs, or whatever the Kentucky native cousin was, could be edible after it was skinned and washed.

Rabbits were a cause for celebration, and after a while, after scaring up some turkeys, they decided that going without any sort of fowl was unacceptable. For the first time since they had left Ann Arbor, they got their guns out. They'd felt the noise was worth the risk, especially since they hadn't seen or heard anybody around in a long time.

"You know, for a quiet computer nerd, you're becoming quite the Boy Scout," Patty teased.

"I wasn't just a computer nerd, you know."

"Oh?"

"I minored in chemistry."

"So you're a chemistry-computer nerd?"

"Yeah."

"So you could make stuff and blow things up then? Turning into Timothy McVeigh, are you?"

"Who? Oh him. No, you just have to understand how a chemical reaction is going to…"

She tuned him out and focused. She noticed flapping as the turkeys started to fly out of their roosts and onto the ground. The buckshot in the shotgun wasn't ideal, she thought, but it would do. She nudged him in the ribs to shut him up and pointed. He smiled, and they crept closer. They were too far off to make the shot, and neither of them had ever hunted turkey before. It didn't take them long to get to where the turkeys had flown down, but they were all gone.

"Must have been too loud," she told Neal.

"Maybe at dark they'll come back here again. If we don't talk and set up in place ahead of time…"

"Want to go fishing?" Patty asked.

"Let's go check the traps first, but yeah, fishing sounds good."

"Ok, I have to get more wood for smoking anyways. That old hickory tree by the creek has some branches that fell off and are dried out."

"Ok, you do that, and I'll fish," Neal said.

"Hey!"

"I'll keep the shotgun with me. Maybe we'll see them at the water like we did the other day."

"Anything's possible," she told him.

He smiled as he thought about it. Anything was possible, and other than convenience being a thing of the past, he was as happy at this moment as he had been staying at home alone playing his video games before the world went dark. They left the roosting tree and checked on the traps. Nothing this morning, so they moved a couple around, baiting one of them with some offal from a previous trap.

The afternoon wore on, and Neal spent some time lazily throwing his line into the water with a grub he found from a rotted-out log. It was getting shredded by the little fish of the river. He was waiting for the larger, darker shape that darted out of the deeper part of the water. He wanted to catch the bigger fish, but the little fish were maddening. They were everywhere. He was about ready to pull the line in when he felt more than saw Patty move beside him, pulling his shotgun up to her shoulder. With her trigger finger she motioned for him to be quiet, and he followed the barrel of the gun to the tall grass across the creek.

A fat deer was approaching through the tall grass of the opposite bank. It lowered its head for a drink when the shotgun went off, startling Neal. The deer thrashed, and Patty almost leapt half the width of the creek before making a large splash. In a few short heartbeats, she'd crossed the remaining part of the creek and had slit the deer's throat. She almost got kicked as its lifeblood quickly escaped.

"Why hunger for *Kentucky Fried Chicken* when you can have fillet mignon? Come help me drag this over and we'll figure out how to gut it."

"Hey, I…" He struggled to hold onto the cane pole that was bent in half. "I think I got something."

§ § §

With the summer heat, they butchered the deer as best as they could and cut the meat into thin strips. They at first laid them flat across the shelf, but when they ran out of room, they tied bigger chunks to pieces of Para-cord and hung them from the top of the teepee. Neal got two or three loads of hickory, as there was enough meat there for them to smoke for days and days and days. They discussed sleeping in shifts just to keep the smoke fire going. Neal was heading back to the deeper part of the woods, the shotgun over his shoulder, when he heard the snap of one of his traps near the river, and then a man's scream. It was almost the loudest thing next to the gunshot that he'd heard in a long while.

Against his better instincts, he started walking towards the trap. He heard someone moving swiftly behind him and he spun, pulling the shotgun into a ready position and then stopped short. Patty had her pistol in her hand, her AK slung over her shoulder. He nodded to her. She matched his pace and they moved silently towards the trap and the cursing man. He was dressed in camouflage, a military print pattern. He'd somehow stepped into one of the conibears, and it'd snapped around his shin.

"Hey, you ok?" Neal called out lamely.

The stranger looked up in shock and fumbled for his gun. Both Patty and Neal already had theirs out, and the sight of them stopped the stranger cold.

"Don't shoot me. I stepped into this trap. It hurts."

"I bet it does. What are you doing out here?" Patty asked.

"Hunting," he said, looking at his bolt action rifle.

"Push that out of the way, by the stock, and I'll get the trap off your leg," Neal said, surprising himself.

The stranger complied, and Neal handed his shotgun to Patty. She holstered her pistol and held the shotgun on the stranger as Neal pulled the setting tool out of his daypack and went to work on the springs.

"Don't move until I get both sets of springs undone and the safeties on."

"That really hurts." The strangers lips were pinched together hard, almost bloodless.

"It'll be better soon. Just hold on." Neal pulled the handles of the tool together and put one spring on the safety clip.

The other kept slipping, making the stranger

cry out in pain. Finally, he got it back enough to get the safety engaged and pulled it off the stranger's leg. He pulled his camo pant leg up and looked at the angry purple marks on his shin and calf before he tried to stand. He fell right back down. Neal stepped back, not wanting to get close or touch the stranger. The man made his way up to one knee and then stood, but he was wobbly. He put his hand out in thanks, but Neal shook his head and took the shotgun from Patty, stepping back.

The stranger took Neal's cold, expressionless face as that of somebody who had done hard things, made hard decisions. His refusal to shake hands told him that he'd been fooled before, and that he was a suspicious type. The final thing he noted was that he re-armed himself and gave himself room to shoot. That was wise. The stranger was a dangerous man, but he saw in Neal everything he admired as well. A smile touched the stranger's lips.

"Hey, thanks. I don't mean no harm. As soon as I can walk, I'll get out of your hair." He wobbled and fell on his butt again, his injured leg not supporting his weight.

"Think we should help him?" Neal asked Patty.

"I don't know."

"You out here alone?"

"Mostly. I have family a couple miles away. That's where I came from. The hunting ranch."

Neal and Patty looked at each other, eyebrows raised.

"Hunting ranch?"

"Yeah, I do guided hog hunts. Thought I'd get some venison today instead of pork chops…" He winced and rubbed his shin.

"You think you're going to be able to walk?"

"Honestly? No. Hobble maybe, in a couple of hours."

Neal handed his shotgun back to Patty, who gave him a fierce look, and he slinged the stranger's gun over his shoulder before helping him up. He fought his warring emotions off and helped the stranger to his feet.

"Let's get you something to drink, and we'll set up a camp out here for you until you're better."

"Neal…" Patty warned.

"Just don't try to follow us back to our place when you can move."

"I don't know how long that's going to take. The leg is swelling."

"Soak it in the cold stream," Patty said. "I'll leave Neal here with you for now and at least re-fill your canteen."

"Here." He dipped it into the stream and then pulled a glass bottle out of a breast pocket and dropped a capsule inside of it. "Purification tablets."

"Neal, don't give him his gun back until I come back with some stuff. I have to check on…you know."

Neal nodded. "Thanks Patty, I'll see you soon."

She headed off into the woods, anger stamped into her features. Neal couldn't help it; she had helped him out in the beginning, and he felt like he needed to pay that debt off and help someone else out. It was part of him coming out of his shell. The stranger held out his hand again.

"Neal, huh? I'm Ken Robertson. Kenny to friends and family."

CHAPTER 12

OUTSIDE THE HOMESTEAD, KENTUCKY

H ere they come," Weston whispered across the trail from Blake.

Two sets of footsteps preceded their legs coming into view from the trail. Both waited, drawing a bead on the targets, having come up with a plan before they'd set up the ambush. They knew the cannies were going to circle around by the conversation they'd overheard, and they'd quickly followed their own trail back to a small valley and took position halfway up one side of the heavily forested area. The plan was for Weston to take the first man out, regardless if it was Marv or Jerry. They didn't know who was who and frankly didn't care. What they needed were answers, and it seemed that these two had decided to hunt them no matter what.

Mentally, they both counted, one, two…The

THE WORLD HUNGERS

shots came from behind them, and Weston flopped on the ground, hitting hard. A wet gasp escaped his lips, and Blake looked at him in shock as two more shots rang out. One hit Blake low in the thigh, the other punching high on his right side. He fell sideways, the pain blossoming, huge, consuming his mind. He hit the ground hard and watched as a red pool formed underneath him on the rich loamy forest ground. He was too weak, couldn't move his head, but he could hear footsteps approaching, excited voices talking, but their words were muted. Three pairs of boots came into his vision, and he almost vomited when he was picked up and thrown over somebody's shoulder.

Everything went hazy at the edges and he struggled for breath. The stranger walked with a limping gait, and the motion made him black out entirely as shock overtook him.

§ § §

Neal awoke with a start. It was the same nightmare again. He moved around, trying to find Patty. The nightmare was a rehashed reality, the absolute horror of the situation overloading his brain. He heard a soft snoring in the utter darkness and inched closer until his hand found hers. He'd gone against his better instincts and helped Ken, sat with him for a day, and then walked him halfway out of their area before giving him his gun back. It wasn't 24 hours later that Neal and Patty had awoken in the middle of the night with Ken and several men pointing guns at them.

They took everything. All the stored food, the books, the tools and supplies. Then, they cuffed Patty and Neal and made them walk out to where an old Ford Truck waited, an hour's walk from the stream. It wasn't until they were all loaded up that they realized that there was seven men all told, many of whom kept shooting glances at Patty and making crude remarks or obscene gestures. The noise and shock of it all almost made Neal withdraw deep into his head. As it was, he was running on autopilot just to survive. Once they got to the hunting lodge, they were ushered past two small buildings to an old smoke house that had been converted into a holding cell. Heavy timber and sheet metal lined the interior, and there were hooks hanging on the wall. Only the old dried bloodstains hinted at what this area was now used for.

That was the reality. In his dreams, the men take Patty from him and do horrible, unspeakable things to her. She always begs and shrieks for Neal to do something. He always responds the same way in the dream that repeats over and over and over and over in his mind, waking him up, causing him to sweat from guilt and fear: *I'm sorry, I just don't feel the same way about things.*

It was the worst thing he'd ever told someone, especially now that he wasn't sure he had meant it. The repetition of it in his dreams and the horrors that woke him up told him one thing: it was a guilt dream, and he did in fact feel the same way she did. It just took him longer to realize it. All sense of night and day had stopped in the absolute darkness, and if they went much longer without food, they would be too weak to fight back when the time came. Neal didn't like that idea, because he suddenly had a lot of fight in him.

Water was something that was going to be the more desperate issue. Bottles of it had been tossed in with them, and then they had been left to their own devices. Time was meaningless in the dark, and only the oppressive heat of the structure gave them a hint that it was daytime. Instead, they used sleep cycles. In the dark, they slept more than not. It was something Neal was used to. He was so used to retreating into his own mind that he often lulled himself into a sudden sleep or nap. He never usually affected his sleep at night, and he often slept more hours in a day than he was awake.

Patty hadn't taken well to the capture. She cried hysterically the first day, more in anger and fear than any real pain. She tried to comfort Neal about him trusting the stranger, telling him that she'd not lost her humanity enough to have wanted to shoot Kenny in cold blood when they found him. It only proved that you couldn't just trust everybody. They certainly hadn't, and a friendly face had turned into an absolute nightmare for the both of them.

The sound of a pickup truck woke Patty, and she bolted upright.

"What was that?" she asked, running her hand

over her forehead to ease the dull headache that had started the day after their water ran out.

"Trucks leaving. Hope they crash."

"Me too," she said softly, sitting up and leaning into Neal's side.

"Maybe it means they'll open up the door. If they do…"

"We fight. We have to. I won't let Kenny have me."

"I won't either," Neal said softly, already knowing the leader's intent for them.

He'd respected Neal enough to not kill him outright, but he'd been fascinated with Patty. He was a widower with a daughter and was looking for a mother for her. He'd given them the basics of his deal while inside the back of the pickup truck on their ride back to the ranch. If Patty became his, Neal could live as a prisoner, unhurt but out of reach. To decline the offer was to be placed on the hooks. They hadn't known what that meant until he put them in the darkness for a while to 'soften' them up and give her a chance to consider his proposition.

They waited in silence until they heard the truck motor come back. Angry voices and shouts from the truck elicited surprised yells from the lodge, and soon there was a flurry of sound. The door was rudely yanked open, and harsh sunlight blinded them both, killing their will to fight. They were manhandled to their feet and dragged towards the lodge, their toes barely touching the ground.

THE WORLD HUNGERS

Two other bloody forms were dragged from the pickup truck.

"Where are you taking us?" Neal asked.

"Shut up," the guy holding his left arm yelled.

"Take them all to the garage," Kenny snarled. His shirt was bloodstained, and he was dragging a half-conscious man. "I want answers."

They were all pushed into the garage through a side door. Only one bay of the garage held a shiny new Suburban that sat dead in the parking space. A quick glance showed them that there was a room split off from the other bay, full of cleaning supplies for the ranch. The bay was bare, with sheetrock nailed in place and lawn furniture piled up on one side. Neal looked at the newcomers, captives like them. One of them had been shot in the side, under the armpit by the look of the bloodstains. The second man had a bullet wound in his leg and his back, possibly near his shoulder blade. Both were pale with pain and blood loss.

§ § §

Blake looked around the room, his eyes half open. It looked like they were bleeding out on floor of an everyday American's garage. Kenny, the man with the limp, pulled a stack of lawn chairs off to the side. He put four of them down against the back wall and indicated to the men to put the prisoners there. Weston groaned but didn't regain consciousness as he slumped in his chair.

135

Patty looked around in a panic. Was this some sort of demonstration of power? She knew in her heart there was no way she'd willingly go to this monster. Not alive. She was pushed into the chair between Blake and Neal, with Weston taking the end spot.

"Now, I've got some questions for you guys, and miss, you already know what I want." He smirked. "Now you two, where is your group situated?" He kicked Blake's bad leg, making him cry out in pain.

Blake screamed, pain overwhelming his senses.

"I said, where is your homestead?"

"It's up in the hills," he panted.

"Good, good. Where in the hills?"

"Up a driveway." He panted and screamed as he was kicked again.

"That's not what I'm asking. Where is your house? What is your address?"

"I don't have one, it's off the grid."

"Maybe I should just kill him?" Marv asked.

"Naw, maybe we should just kill his friend?" Jerry piped up, his crossbow starting to rise.

"Now there's an interesting thought," Kenny said, pulling out a large hunting knife. "Where is your homestead?"

"Fucking cannibal," Blake spat back.

There was a pregnant silence. Patty and Neal looked at the group holding them hostage with something like shock.

"Cannibals? Only selectively. There's enough game here to keep us fed for a while."

THE WORLD HUNGERS

"Yeah, eating the hearts gives us strength over our—"

"Shut up, Marv," Jerry said, jabbing his elbow into the smaller man's side.

The others in Kenny's group looked a little green at that thought, and they looked at the leader and the two trackers with something like horror and disgust.

"Oh, cannibalism has been practiced as long as there has been mankind. I've never fed you guys human flesh," he told his gang. "Unless they asked for it." He looked to Marv and Jerry.

"That's...that's sick," Patty told them.

"It's only been two months since the power went out. Surly you weren't starving?" Neal asked, the horror of the situation dawning on him.

"Oh, it's more like getting bored with the same old, same old. In a backwoods hunt in Africa, I learned about the practice from the local tribal leader. They ate the heart and livers of their victims to gain the courage and power of the fallen warriors. I tried it, wasn't bad. Now that we are selectively thinning the herd in our area, I wondered what it'd be like. So here we are. Answer my question, because I want to know what kind of sheep are in my meadows."

"What do you want to know?" Neal asked, ready to tell him anything.

Kenny smiled, a wicked gleam in his eye. With a start, the captives realized that they weren't dealing with a sane man, and perhaps fear or security was the only thing keeping the nervous men he surrounded himself with there with him in this den of insanity.

"I want to know where his group is from. You aren't a part of it, are you?" He pointed his knife at Neal, before using the flat of the blade to tilt his chin up.

"No, I'm not. We came in from Ann Arbor."

A low whistle answered this. Kenny moved over to Patty, and he slid the blade under the straps of one side of her bra and tank top and slit it. The fabric parted easily, falling halfway down her shoulder before stopping at the cup of her bra.

"Is that true, missy?" He ran the tip of the knife across the bottom of her throat gently, drawing a bead of blood at the junction of her chest and neck before stopping its movement under the other side of her straps.

"Yes, we lived by the university. We were neighbors. I have my ID…"

Kenny slit the fabric, watching it fall, probably expecting her bra to fall loose. His eyes widened in anticipation, but he'd forgotten about the back strap. He made up for it by putting his hand on her neck, using his thumb to gently rub her lips. She froze and held still until Kenny moved in front of Blake. He didn't try to threaten him, just asked him a question, quietly.

"Where is your group?"

"Go to hell," Blake told him defiantly, his head wobbling as he tried to look the other man in the

THE WORLD HUNGERS

eye.

The knife flashed and Blake flinched. It sank up to its hilt in Weston's sternum, then Kenny ripped it up savagely. Weston jerked for a moment, a small spray of blood coming out of his mouth before Blake screamed obscenities. He wiped the blade off on Weston's shirt and stood in front of Blake again.

"One last time, where is your homestead?" He held the blade at Blake's throat.

Neal was so shocked that he was nearly comatose, but he'd gotten an idea. If it worked out, he could maybe save the stranger as well as Patty and himself. The logical side of his brain was trying to calculate the odds of survival of this crazy plan, but no matter how many chips were stacked against them, the plan was the only chance at survival he saw.

"Ken, stop. I'll make a deal with you," Neal shouted.

The knife wavered for a moment and then Ken turned to look, a crazed expression on his face.

"Go on?" He gestured with his knife.

"I'll make you a trade," Neal said.

"For what?"

"I'll have Patty come with you willingly, and you let us guys go."

"What?" The look of shock and disgust matched her horrified expression. "Neal, how could you?"

Neal swallowed, and for once he was thankful that he couldn't show his emotions well.

"You were a great neighbor and friend, but I

139

don't like you the same way you like me. Sorry."

"You…you…" She broke down in tears.

"Free? Go free?" He looked at Patty, taking in her curves with his hungry eyes, her hair that fell like golden strands of silk, the natural beauty that shone through despite her being dirty, grimy, and without a wash for days on end while they were locked up.

"I just have to convince her. Let me talk to her."

"No."

"It's the only way I can convince her."

"You're sure you can?" He licked his lips.

"What are you doing, Kenny?" one of his men asked, one of the group who had been horrified when he found out his leader was consuming human flesh.

"Don't worry about it," he snapped.

"Let me talk to her. Alone," Neal said, knowing it was a gamble, and if he lost the throw of the dice…

"Ok, put them in the storage room. You have two minutes."

"That's all I'll need."

He stood and tried to take Patty's hand. She pulled her arm away from him and tried to look away.

"If she won't go with you, I'll carry her myself." Ken rubbed himself, smiling broadly.

He played with his knife a second, and Patty broke under his intense gaze and jumped to her feet and stalked away from Neal. He followed her into the supply room and almost cringed at the angry, hurt expression on her face.

"Remember, two minutes to convince her to come willingly."

"I'd rather die!" she snarled, but they were shutting the door.

"I can't believe I ever felt—" she started screaming, but Neal stepped in close and shut her mouth with a passionate kiss.

He ran his fingers through the sides of her hair, and when her breath hitched, he pulled back.

"I love you. We don't have much time, you have to trust me, ok?" His voice was almost lost in the shock that Patty felt.

"What?" She looked punch-drunk and confused.

"Get those buckets out for me. Hurry."

Neal ran to the shelving units and found a large bottle of ammonia and a bottle of bleach. When he turned, something else caught his eye. It was a package of pool chlorine and shock in the powdered form. He shoved that in his pocket and turned to find that Patty had grabbed four pails. She was holding them out.

"You almost done in there?" a loud voice boomed out from the other side of the door.

"I still have ninety seconds," Neal yelled back. He was rewarded with a laugh.

"Don't break her."

"I'll break all of you," he muttered. Taking two of the buckets, he tore the cap off the bleach and poured the gallon of it between two of the buckets.

"What are you doing?"

"Arming ourselves." He took the other two buckets and poured the ammonia. The smell hit them right away, sharp and pungent.

"Hold your breath, and then throw this on them."

"Hold my breath?"

"Bleach plus ammonia makes hydrochloric acid and chlorine gas. It's deadly. Now. Hold your breath now." He poured the bleach into the bucket of ammonia and motioned her to do the same.

He almost kicked the door off its hinges getting it open. Two of Kenny's men, the trackers, were right there by the jam, trying to listen in with Kenny standing a few feet behind them. Neal flung the bubbling gassing liquid on all three. The two in the front caught it full on the chest and face, and Kenny caught the splatter on the side of his head. They screamed in horror. Neal took the bucket from Patty and waited until the others came running to the doorway to check on them. He flung the volatile mess at them, hitting them in the chest with the caustic liquid. Marv and Jerry fell to the ground, their exposed skin sloughing off in strips as the men choked and gagged.

Neal took Patty's hand and pulled her to where the remaining wounded prisoner was. They each took an experimental breath and almost gasped. Blake was also having a hard time breathing, and they only slowed their way to the door to grab a

THE WORLD HUNGERS

shotgun from one of Kenny's men. The coughs and wet gasps from Kenny's gang filled the air as they thrashed on the concrete.

"Hurry, Ken's gone," Neal gasped.

Pushing the door open to the outside was a literal breath of fresh air, and Blake staggered, his bad leg not supporting his weight. A door to the house slammed shut, and they half dragged, half walked Blake between them towards the trucks. They pushed him in the side door of the Ford. Luckily, the keys were in the ignition.

"I can't drive," Neal told Patty. "I never learned."

"I can, unless it's a stick," she said.

"It is," Blake told them, moving into the driver's seat. "Get in."

Patty slid in and felt a tap on her right shoulder. She turned and saw Neal looking in at her.

"I do love you. I wasn't lying. I need to disable the other truck. If I don't make it…"

"Just hurry," she said, tears welling up in her eyes.

Neal ran, pulling the packet of pool shock from his pocket and tearing it open. He slid to a stop next to the bed and pulled the fuel door open. He dropped the gas cap as he heard a gunshot ring out. He ducked, dropping the packet. He got on his knees and scooped up the packet and poured it down the fuel port. It was an older truck, and the crystals easily slid down the opening. He ran as low to the ground as he could, keeping the truck's body between him and Patty before he leapt into the bed of the pickup.

"Go!" he yelled, just as another gunshot rang out.

They tore out of the long drive of the hunting ranch just as a fire erupted from the truck, engulfing it in flames.

"I'm Blake," a bloody, wincing driver told Patty.

"I'm Patty, that's Neal." She nodded to the bed of the truck. "Where are we going?"

"To my homestead. We have shelter, defenses, and safety."

"Let's go."

CHAPTER 13

THE HOMESTEAD, KENTUCKY

Blake laid on the horn as he was coming up the driveway. Stealth was gone, and he knew if he passed out before his family could find him, the newcomers would die in the traps and defenses. Duncan stepped out from his vantage point, an M4 held at the ready. His body shook with tension. Blake's vision wavered and he came to a dead stop as he stalled the truck, finally passing out.

"Blake," Duncan shouted as he approached the truck. He yelled to Bobby over his shoulder.

Bobby stepped out of the gloom on the east side of the lane, surprising Patty as he opened the passenger door, a pistol in his fist. He quickly pulled the shotgun from Patty's limp hands, and she half turned to check on Neal to make sure he wasn't go-

145

ing to freak out. There was no movement she could see from the bed of the truck, and she began to rise when Bobby pushed her back gently.

"Get Blake out of here," Duncan said.

Bobby nodded and picked up Blake in a fireman's carry. He hustled up the hill and out of sight. Duncan raised the radio to his lips.

"I've got one wounded, send the quad. Blake's priority number one. I'm not sure if the stranger here is going to make it."

Patty looked around in shock, startling Duncan, who dropped the radio and raised the M4, pointing it at her head.

"Hold still, easy. Where's Weston?" His gun wavered slightly.

"Neal, is he ok?" Her voice was strained and her body shook from fear and tension as she stared into the bore of the carbine.

"Where is Weston?" he repeated. "Is that Neal in the back?"

"Yes, he's...let me see him."

"Ma'am, you better not," Duncan told her.

"No, I have to." She ignored the gun and almost pulled the door handle off as a sob escaped her lips. She jumped in the bed of the truck where Neal was. Blood was coming out of his nose and mouth, and a neat hole in the fabric of his shirt bubbled, air in the blood.

"No...Neal, Neal honey, just hold on," she sobbed, holding her hand on the ghastly wound.

Duncan saw her reaction and knew in his heart

that she was no threat. She was disarmed and going to pieces over the man whose lungs had been torn apart by a bullet. Still, he could try.

"Pull him to the edge, follow me. There are traps everywhere. Step where I step, do you got it?"

She nodded, the world a blur. She cried harder when she saw his back, a larger hole exited just below his shoulder blade, and his entire back was scarlet. The portly pastor cradled the small man and started walking. Time almost stood still for Patty when three quads showed up, two of the drivers were women, the other was the young man from earlier.

"Put him on with me," Bobby screamed, and a gasping Duncan did so, not having enough breath to acknowledge.

Duncan climbed on one of the quads behind a woman, clutching his heart, and the two women drivers exchanged worried glances.

"You get on with me hun," a fierce-looking woman said to Patty.

Bobby kept one hand around the unconscious man with his left arm and muscled the quad with his right. The Four-Trax had an automatic transmission, so he was able to steer and use the throttle, though his arm would later be almost too sore to move.

They pulled to the house, where Martha was already set up. She was fussing over Blake when they arrived, and both Lisa and Karen took Duncan under the arms and helped him walk into the house.

BOYD CRAVEN

Patty followed Bobby, who was carrying Neal. A tiny woman with short hair was crying over the man they'd saved from Kenny. A little boy held his hand as the other woman cut away his jacket. A bandage had already been tied across his pant-less leg. She looked up and saw the others come in.

"Blake's going to be fine. He's in shock; get fluids going," she shouted to a tearful Lisa. Lisa looked between Duncan and Martha before leaving her husband.

"Karen, get Duncan lying down flat on his back. Then go get my bag that's on the porch."

"I'm ok. It isn't that bad," Duncan gasped.

"Just do it."

The woman hurried off and Patty watched, helpless as Neal was set up, held in place by another woman, who was pressing a gauze wad to the hole in his lower back. Martha took one look at Neal and felt his pulse. She gave a worried look to the wounded stranger and the new woman and pulled his eyelid open. Neal stirred for a moment, his eyes focusing on Patty.

"I do love you. I really do…" he said as his eyes closed for the last time.

Patty pulled him close, not believing, not wanting to believe it, not capable of believing it, not accepting it, and she called his name over and over and over as they worked.

Karen returned and Martha shoved two pills in Duncan's mouth, who gagged, then dry swallowed. She then put one under his tongue and told him to hold it. She turned to Lisa and told her to pray she got the dosage right, she wasn't a medical doctor. Almost immediately Duncan's face relaxed, and his breathing evened out.

"Told you I was ok," he said again. "Easier this time." Duncan told his wife.

Lisa ran her hands through his hair. Patty took in the chaos as it happened around her. Seconds turned to minutes, minutes added up, and still she held onto Neal until a crying little boy pulled on her shoulder.

"Please lady, come help me. My mommy can't. She's with Daddy," Chris told her.

Reluctantly she let herself be pulled away and towards the kitchen.

"Where's my son, where's Weston?" Lisa asked.

Patty paused and turned to look at the woman, taking in her features.

"Was he the guy with Blake?"

Lisa stiffened, immediately noticing how the young woman had used the past tense.

"Yes..." she said in a quiet voice.

"He wasn't in the truck with them," Duncan said.

"The guy from the hunting ranch, he murdered him," Patty told her.

Just then, the base radio that was installed in the living room squeaked, and a voice came out of the speaker.

"David, this is Gerard, come in? David, this is Gerard. Orders have changed and our detachment will be swinging by your way in one week, do you copy?"

—*THE END*—

ABOUT THE AUTHOR

Boyd Craven III was born and raised in Michigan, an avid outdoors-man who's always loved to read and write from a young age. When he isn't working outside on the farm, or chasing a household of kids, he's sitting in his Lazy Boy, typing away.

http://www.boydcraven.com/
Facebook: https://www.facebook.com/boydcraven3
Email: boyd3@live.com
You can find the rest of Boyd's books on Amazon:
http://www.amazon.com/-/e/B00BANIQLG

38225041R00097

Made in the USA
San Bernardino, CA
01 September 2016